OUR FATAL
MAGIC

Our Fatal Magic by Tai Shani
First published by Strange Attractor Press, 2019
ISBN: 9781907222818

Introduction © Bridget Crone 2019
Cover illustration 'Heaty' by Allison Katz
'Our Fatal Magic' typography by Eleanor Edwards
Layout by Jamie Sutcliffe

Strange Attractor Press
BM SAP, London,
WC1N 3XX, UK
www.strangeattractor.co.uk

Distributed by The MIT Press, Cambridge, Massachusetts.
And London, England
Printed and bound in the UK by TJ International

OUR FATAL
MAGIC

TAI SHANI

Collected Texts from DC: Semiramis

NOTE

Our Fatal Magic is a collection of fragmentary fictions that were presented as monologues during the project *DC: Semiramis*, an expanded adaptation of Christine de Pizan's 1405 proto-feminist text, *The Book of the City of Ladies*. It took place over four years and was iterated through interconnected yet stand-alone performances, installations and films of monologue texts which represented the various characters in the adaptation. In 2018, *DC: Semiramis* culminated in a large-scale, sculptural, immersive installation that also functioned as a site for a twelve-part performance series, presented over four days. Each episode focused on one of the characters from an allegorical post-patriarchal city.

Elements of this collection have previously appeared in:
Buried
The Bodies That Remain, Punctum Press
On Violence, Ma Bibliotheque
Self Love, *Eros Journal*, Eros Press
The Happy Hypocrite, Book Works

CONTENTS

INTRODUCTION

WOUNDS OF UN-BECOMING

BRIDGET CRONE

Tai Shani's *DC: Semiramis* is an epic project comprising performance, the exhibition of related sculptural, sonic and video works, and the twelve interrelated texts upon which they are based published here for the first time as *Our Fatal Magic*. *Our Fatal Magic* is thus the final manifestation of a five-year project that has taken many forms. Weaving together inspiration from a diverse field of feminist and proto-feminist literature – from Christine de Pizan's *City of Women* published in 1405 to more contemporary feminist science fiction such as Marge Piercy's *Woman on the Edge of Time* (1976) and Pamela Sargeant's *The Shore of Women* (1986) – *DC: Semiramis* lays the ground for a place apart, a city for women, a feminist space, a room of one's own. This place apart is the land of Semiramis, warrior queen of ancient history, myth and legend, but also that 'dark continent' Sigmund Freud referred to as the unknown terrain of the 'sexuality of adult women'.[1] *DC: Semiramis* is

1 Freud quoted in Mary Ann Doane, *Femmes Fatales: Feminism,*

therefore a space-time that is both mythical and historical, a world built by and for women that is defined by their confinement and perceived threat. It is also the city that Pizan builds, the city for which she names the first stone Semiramis. (*City of Women*: Book II)

It is important to note from the outset that Shani builds her city anew, so that rather than laying claim to an existing city with citizenry pre-defined, she aims for an expansive and inclusive space. In so doing, Shani engages in the riskier and more complex project of examining the very constitution of the city itself. Embodiment, voice and self are at stake here, as is the question of what might be considered 'feminine' – the descriptor for a set of tropes that we first see delineated in Pizan's *City*. In *Our Fatal Magic* and the *DC: Semiramis* project as a whole, the 'feminine' is mobilised to describe the production of the body through particular experiences in and of the world.[2]

Film Theory, Psychoanalysis. (London and New York: Routledge, 1991): 210.

2 In many ways, it would be more useful to write 'feminine*', echoing the use of 'trans*' by trans theorists and activists who use 'trans*' to indicate the broad possibilities of gender expression beyond any biological or essentialist (or cis) notions of gender. In particular, reese simpkins recognises the embodied and material processes of becoming indicated by 'trans*', where the body itself is never a given but always in a process of materialisation. (reese simpkins, 'Temporal Flesh, Material Becomings.') In other words, like 'trans*', 'feminine*' could be used to signal to a body that is always-already in a transitional state; that is a state of becoming that is inflected by experiences in and of the world. In referencing the work of trans* theorists in this way, I want to emphasise that I am not making a direct equivalence between the complexities of trans* experience and that of cis bodies (and in this way emptying

Here the feminine describes a mode of inhabiting the world, and the way in which a world acts to shape a body. And so, we might ask which bodies inhabit the world of *DC: Semiramis*? On what basis – through which acts of coding or encoding – are these bodies materialised? For in the world of *DC: Semiramis*, it is violence that possesses this formative power of constitution and inclusion. What does it mean to belong, and thus to delineate and collectivise experience in this way? This collective organisation of bodies is exemplified by the walls that surround Pizan's *The City of Women*, and likewise by the delineation of the space of the stage in the performance version of Shani's *DC: Semiramis*. The city and the stage each act as a border that differentiates between the inside and outside. It thus organises inhabitants, actors and citizens inside its bounds and excludes those outside. The bodies that materialise in the world of *DC: Semiramis*, bound by the city of women, are diverse and self-defined – trans*, differently abled, of different ages, sizes and shapes. At the same time (and complicating things further), while the texts that make up *Our Fatal Magic* deal with questions concerning the formation of the body through violence, the work also

---

the rich nuance and urgency from this work in the field of trans studies), and thus will use 'feminine' and not 'feminine*' in this essay to respect the specificity of this work. However, as Susan Styker and others have pointed out, the 'trans*' experience highlights the formative precarity of all gendered experience / bodies, and my use of 'feminine' should be recognised within this context and of what Stryker has elsewhere referred to as the 'transgender phenomenon' which lays bare the *unnaturalness of all gender*. (Stryker 'Biopolitics': 40)

addresses the violent dismantling of this very same body. Predominant then are not only the processes of becoming but also those of *un-becoming*; un-becoming as both an unravelling of the body-subject and an extension beyond it towards some other state of being or not-being. This is a battle which Shani elicits, of being or becoming a body, and at the same time escaping its confinement towards some other freer, more ecstatic state.

Evoking Pizan's pre-Enlightenment, proto-feminist text, *The City of Women* as an inspiration for *DC: Semiramis* has the effect of conjoining the struggle for the self-constitution, value and recognition of women's power (Pizan uses the term 'ability') with more contemporary questions concerning the very constitution of the human. It is the presence of Pizan's text in relation to *DC: Semiramis* (and its ritualised violence) that opens up a sense of the almost barbaric fragility or precarity of the feminine. For while there is a valorisation of a women's voice (knowledges, language and so on) and a demonstration of feminine skills and virtues in Pizan's text, this 'femininity' is something that must be called forth against a backdrop of funerals, tournaments, violent seductions, abandonment and so on. Therefore, it is at once fixed through an expression of rigid gender roles and social conventions and, at the same time, fragile and subject to threat as the result of these very same boundaries. In Shani's work, this violence is present as both the violent struggle to have voice (recognition, representation) and the violence that threatens voice and ultimately self-constitution. Violence thus appears as both a forming and formative force that shapes the body, albeit precariously at times, while at others this violence is seized upon in defiance; it is possessed and inflicted by the 'feminine' as self-authoring, as pleasure and as self-pleasuring. In this way, violence acts to shape the body in *DC: Semiramis* – shaping it materially – suggesting the body as a malleable form that can be thus transformed.

Shani's concern is therefore not only with the emergence of a kind of proto-feminism within Pizan's fifteenth-century context, but also with the question of what constitutes the body now. How might a body be organised in relation to other bodies? And, finally, how might we escape its confines (once established)? Translated more abstractly, this is firstly the question of what it is to have or be a body and what this might mean *materially* – that is, what form a body might take. Secondly, it is the question of how this body is then organised or represented in relation to other bodies. Another simpler way of expressing this question of organisation and delineation is to simply ask: what constitutes the feminine? It is this question that demands a broader address and *queering* to approach gender beyond the binarism of Pizan and some of the other works of feminist science fiction (for example Sargeant) to which Shani refers, in order to expand the bounds of the feminine. The suggestion here is to think from *DC: Semiramis* towards a messier and more agonistic model of gender that moves beyond the binarism of Pizan (where 'woman' is an existing category that battles to be recognised) or the neutrality of Piercy (where gender binarism is neatly managed and politely interchangeable). And finally, once this body emerges (complicatedly feminine, as noted earlier) in and through the world, we approach the third question: what are the possibilities for escape from the confinement of this body, both materially and psychically? That is to say, in asking what is being, we must also be prepared to entertain the question of what is not-being.

To understand the body, and particularly the gendered body, in relation to states of emergence is to understand the body and gender as a part of an ongoing material process rather than 'the alignment of a signifying sex (male or female) with a signified social category (man or woman) or psychical disposition (masculine or feminine).'[3] Here the body can be understood as 'biopolitical' (echoing Foucault) or what Joseph Pugliese and Susan Stryker term a 'somatechnical assemblage' – that is, a body that is produced through the nexus of its embodied experiences in the world and the technical and biopolitical constitution of that body, whether chemical, hormonal, environmental, geographic, financial or political. In this way, the body, and indeed embodiment, 'is always biocultural, always techno-organic, always a practical achievement realized through some concrete means.'[4] This is of course in direct contrast to the medieval proto-feminist basis for *DC: Semiramis* and the manner in which Pizan has been understood as 'a defender of her sex' as well as offering instruction in virtuous behaviour to that so-called sex – where this 'sex' is defined

3   Susan Stryker, 'Biopolitics' in *Trans Studies Quarterly* 1.1-2 (2014): 39.

4   Joseph Pugliese and Susan Stryker, 'The Somatechnics of Race and Whiteness' in *Social Semiotics* 19.1 (2009): 2.

as a series of fixed rules or qualities.[5] Yet in the texts that make up *DC: Semiramis*, reference to Pizan is overtaken by a voice that is both diaristic and full of fantasy – a voice that combines violent experience with violent fantasy. This has the effect of enacting a form of hyberbolic fictioning such that gender itself is highlighted as a series of rules (Pizan's feminine virtues, for example), experiences and productions *that could be otherwise* and that are themselves formed under duress – materially shaped rather than 'given'. It is for this reason that *DC: Semiramis* must be seen to address the body in a process of un-becoming as much as it is in a state of becoming. Threatened with violence (and sometimes seeking that violence or enacting it), there is a precarity here of a body in a two-way process of becoming and un-becoming – that is, a body torn between emergence and disappearance, between production and dismemberment, between production and de-production.

In *Our Fatal Magic* it is the wound or the cut that produces the portal that enables the double movement between becoming and un-becoming. 'The first cut is the deepest' (as lamented by P.P. Arnold) is the refrain repeated across all 12 chapters of *Our Fatal Magic,* providing an exit from the conditions imposed upon the body; an exit that takes place through the body itself. And, in this way, the cut is always more than symbolic: operating as a material process of the body *stretched* and *extended* towards another

5 Rosalind Brown-Grant, 'Introduction' in Christine de Pizan, *The Book of the City of Ladies*. (Penguin Classics, 1999, Kindle Edition): loc.663.

possibility, it is also productive. It is, as such, the rent or tear through which the body is produced through the folding of external forces upon the flesh. In other words, the wound or the cut is an interface of, or for, 'technosomatic assemblage' because it is a refrain that folds inside out and outside in.[6] It is this connective passage – portal, wormhole – that projects or spews forth the body's interior fleshly pains and joys, while folding its interactions back across and through the flesh. The cut is thus a site of constant production. And thus for Shani, writing is also produced through the cut; it is pushed out through the tangible, painful labour of the body – the body that *writes* itself. 'The first cut is the deepest' thus cuts into the body, but also into the body of the text, cleaving away a space for the emergence of text (more text) and acting to bind the 12 chapters together into a whole (a body itself). This has the effect of producing a body that is itself written through the text and a text that is written through the body. Here, writing is an embodied practice pushed out through fingertips, through the wound of the mouth; perhaps birthed, cut or torn from – at the very least orgasmed or otherwise ejaculated through – the fleshy folds of the labouring body.[7]

6   Stryker, 'Biopolitics': 40. Pugliese and Stryker, 'The Somatechnics of Race and Whiteness': 2.

7 Shani has written of the difficult experience of writing or of coming to write. In an interview with curator Laura Hensser, Shani states:

> It's quite interesting because I feel writing is what I'm good at, though I don't find it easy at all. I actually find it really torturous and quite arduous; it takes a lot out of me. I can't just sit and write... You mentioned earlier that maybe this work could go

The exhibited and performed iterations of the *DC:Semiramis* project unfold upon or around a landscape of bodies that includes a giant hand that holds a human form, a large globular structure with a televisual eye, pieces of meat-stone, a flesh-coloured snake-like form amongst various crystals and other icons. In fact, when viewing the stage face-on, the collected objects are arranged to form a face of sorts. This is not only a gesture towards understanding the process of embodiment as a form of body-to-body or body-upon-body circuitry, represented through the emergence of a body within a landscape of bodies, but also a reference to a particular set of influences from pornographic film to B-movies. These include Japanese 'pink film' of the 1960s such as Yazuso Masumura's *Blind Beast* (1969) in which the protagonist Aki becomes trapped in a world of bodies sculpted by her captor, the blind sculptor Michio. In the film, Aki gradually succumbs to the world in which she has become entrapped as it becomes an endless world from which escape becomes less and less viable. As Aki enters into the totality of this strange world-of-bodies, her captor Michio also becomes trapped in the bodily circuitry, such that the two end up devouring each other – literally cutting or ripping into each other's flesh. While there is no question that Aki is Michio's victim (she is after all kidnapped and held captive by Michio with the aid of his mother), there

---

on forever, I don't feel that way anymore. It could theoretically, but I don't necessarily want that. It could, in a way, evolve or become something different but these really intense, internal monologues are painful and exhausting. http://www.objektiv.no/realises/2018/5/7/tai-shani

is also a sense in the film of both protagonists seeking a freedom from the strict cultural and social mores of post-War Japanese society. In this way, the accelerating violence of Aki and Michio's passion (echoed in other films of the period such as Nagisa Oshima's *In the Realm of the Senses* (1976)) becomes a means for escape into a realm that extends the body towards another bodily state or modality, and towards another language or form of expression. Thus the violence to which Aki and Michio succumb acts to emphasise a purely bodily, somatic state – a body to body transmission, a world of extreme feeling and affect that is echoed in both *DC: Semiramis* and *Our Fatal Magic*. As Shani writes in Chapter 3: Paradise: 'I will not use your language again'.

The setting of *Our Fatal Magic* within the terrain of the body is also signalled through the use of watery, liquid imagery, particularly in the video translation of the third chapter, Paradise. This video opens with a sweeping bird's-eye view of the surface of the ocean, a shot that signals towards the vast, wholistic oneness of the sea. Waves begin to crash violently against rocks and our view shifts from that of an overview to a close-up, immersing us in water and then suddenly into blood, as blood-red plasma begins to fill the screen. The effect of this passage is a move from the master image (or overview) – the mastering and mapping image, such as we might find in the case of an aeronautical survey for example – to the molecular view, the close-up, the seeing of things in movement and in-formation. We see this shift mapped in the video, from the overview that is accompanied by a voiceover, stating: 'You have organised this violence', towards a more metabolic and liquid relation that is referred to as 'a basic language' – a language of the body and its feelings, of processes of embodiment and change, of inhabitation. Thus, this passage in *DC: Semiramis* gives one of the strongest indications of the type of viewpoint that we – the viewer, the reader, the interlocuter – are to take within the fabric of the work. For here a clear shift is enacted, from an image that we stand apart from and look upon, to one in which another more bodily view is invited. We see this in the written text of *Our Fatal Magic*, enacted in the move from the 'organising violence' of narrative and the refutation of this language for something other – a 'private, basic' language of the body that is a language of the molecular view, the liquid (blood) relation.

This watery imagery introduces the notion of a liquid relation between bodies, whereby bodies are not segmented and individual but connective and dynamic in their interconnection. Yet threat is never far away in the world of *DC: Semiramis*, and here the interconnectedness that is suggested by the watery 'wholeness' of the ocean is violently 'cut' or cut into with the plasma imagery mentioned earlier and an acceleration of the violence voiced in the accompanying text. Thus the feminist 'hydrology' that is inscribed through this watery relation of bodies raises questions of empathy and shared feeling, particularly in this context of violence (the cut, the wound and the segue from water to blood, in the video), so that we are led to ask what it is to feel? What is it to feel the pain or suffering of another? 'Are you receiving my open eye signal?' the AI, Algealux II, asks us in Paradise.[8] And, by association, we might ask: What it is to feel empathy in the age of computation? Who feels, and how? Who receives the bodily transmissions, the 'open eye signals' of those in another time and space or with a very different experience of the world to their own? The cut or the wound acts as a hinge here too in opening up a passage through these questions of empathy, a theme that is also explored in much feminist science fiction, from Marge Piercy's already cited novel, *Woman On The Edge Of Time*, in which the protagonist Connie is a 'catcher' who receives communication from, and travels to, a future world through her intense connection with someone of that world, to Octavia Butler's *Parable of the Sower* in which the narrator, Lauren, is a 'feeler', her empathetic response is so strong that she feels the pain of others acutely and physically (not metaphorically). In these narratives, empathy becomes a tunnel or portal that cuts into the body, connecting it (sometimes violently) to other bodies and other temporalities. In invoking the question of empathy in relation to the AI, Algealux II, Shani extends the question of feeling and the relationality of empathy beyond the human to ask whether empathy might provide a conduit that connects through screens, through different

---

8 Three AI protagonists appear in the texts that make up the *DC: Semiramis* project: Mnemesoid (an open source software programme that appears in Chapter 10: Mnemesoid), the 'therapeutic AI' named Algealux II in Chapter 3: Paradise), and Psy Chic Anem One (who appears in all episodes as well as its own, Chapter 12: Psy Chic Anem One).

states of being. What role might liveness or presence play in such circuitries?[9]

Following the figure of the empath or 'feeler', or 'catcher', in these examples, to empathise is to feel both outside of the bounds of the present and outside of a linear logic, and thus extends the bounds of empathy as it is commonly understood. While empathy is indeed causal for the empath (as we see in *Parable of the Sower*, Lauren sees the pain of another and then feels it), it also escapes cause into a new temporality, a duration of feeling that haunts the subject and opens the body and subject up to other experiences. Empathy thus enacts a form of time-travel in its haunting of the subject: this is, of course, a haunting that both precedes (as it does for Lauren in *Parable of the Sower*) or exceeds the present moment (as we see in Piercy's *Woman on the Edge of Time*, for example). In its potential for binding across time and space, empathy transmits questions of relation, drawing together a 'we' through the force of affect. It produces a community based on bodily feeling. Yet in producing this 'we' through empathy – that is, through affect – the body reveals its very precarity. It becomes a transmission, a communication or a feeling

9 The translation of *DC: Semiramis* across several formats from the texts published here to the live performance of the work at Glasgow International Festival 2018 and Nottingham Contemporary 2019 to the exhibition of the work across several forms – as video, sound and sculptural installation – suggests that Shani is exploring this very question through the work itself. What is the qualitive space between these different modalities of production, presentation and reception? How do we account for these differences and their potential?

that stretches through the body and between bodies. It produces a body that is porous – open to de-composition as much as composition. As Algealux II states: 'You rained fractals through me'. For in the logic of the empath, to feel someone or something is to open the body as a portal to another possibility, another dimension, an alternate world. But how durable is this transmission and who does it reach? Who does it draw into its walls (to return to Christine de Pizan's *City*) and on what grounds? Can an empathic or affective community replace a gendered one?

In the video works that make up *DC: Semiramis*, the question of address and the relation of bodies produced by this address is felt acutely. This is because Shani plays not only with voice in the narrative content of the work but also in its form. We are, at times, addressed violently from the screen, and, at other times, addressed as if we ourselves are the perpetrators of that violence. This further complicates any thinking about empathy and collectivity: in other words, it complicates the boundaries of the 'we'. 'We are the vision and we are the touch', Shani's character Psy Chic Anem tells us in Chapter Twelve. In response, we might ask: *Who am I that you see, that you touch, Psy Chic Anem One? Who am I that you address, reaching out to you through the screen? Am I you? Or am I John Kramer, your harasser? Am I like you with orifices violated? In responding to your address from the screen, do I become you? Do I become like you, also bloody and salty to taste?* In thinking about the subjective composition of the body and its material production or formation, we must cast our net beyond dimorphisms of all kinds. This means, of course, thinking beyond a binarism of gender but also being prepared to think beyond the positions of subject and object, on-screen or off-, addressor and addressee. It means breaking down the dichotomies of being in the spotlight of the stage or in the steady comfort of Pizan's city walls; it means breaking down these dichotomies to move instead towards a fragmented fractal, molecular or affective connection that re- and de-composes the body in a myriad of forms, through myriad encounters, and through a polyphony of address and response. This is not to suggest that violence does not initially play out along patriarchal gendered lines, but to constantly remake these lines with new allies and new constituents, recognising the potential for new forms of collectivity that emerge through the sensible (the body's capacity for feeling and affect), and to build new worlds of self-hood and sociality through these alliances that lie at the heart of Shani's project.

The cut is crucial here, acting as it does, as a break into the world and as a portal into another state of being. If we think of the role of the empath in much of the feminist science fiction that Shani draws upon, we see empathy stretching beyond the present towards past and future, literally stretching time itself through the action of the cut and of the repeated refrain of violence. 'This is my fatal magic, ok, the first cut is the deepest', is the refrain that is repeated across all twelve chapters of *Our Fatal Magic*. It is this repetition that produces the very possibility of 'fatal magic' in the world of *DC: Semiramis* – a shared world of self-constitution, dissolution, being, being-together, becoming and unbecoming. And as we've seen, the cut produces an entry into another state, inducing both the writing of the text and the world of the text itself;, drawing us into its wound and world. Thus it breaks and produces anew. In calling forth the world of *DC: Semiramis*, it dismantles another world; undoing one narrative for another, unravelling the confines of language and its coding for another, such that becoming is constant but constantly threatened in its very productivity. For to do and to be is also to face the possibility of not doing and not being. Terrifying and glorious at once, for what could we be? This is the 'fatal magic' of *DC: Semiramis*: the force of being in the face of not-being, the sheer effort to be in the face of the world, and to be beyond being. Becoming and unbecoming and becoming beyond the self: 'The first cut is the deepest', she states. This wound of (un)becoming.

REFERENCES

Octavia Butler, *Parable of the Sower*, Headline: Kindle Edition, 2014.

Rosalind Brown-Grant, 'Introduction' in Christine de Pizan, *The Book of the City of Ladies*. Penguin Classics: Kindle Edition, 1999.

Jane Chance, 'Christine de Pizan as Literary Mother: Women's Authority and Subjectivity in 'The Fleure and the Leafe' and 'The Assembly of Ladies'' in Margaret Zimmerman and Dine De Rentis eds. *The City of Scholars: New Approaches to Christine de Pizan*. Berlin and New York: Walter de Gruyter, 1994: 245-259.

Mary Ann Doane, *Femmes Fatales: Feminism, Film Theory, Psychoanalysis*. London and New York: Routledge, 1991.

Joseph Pugliese and Susan Stryker, 'The Somatechnics of Race and Whiteness' in *Social Semiotics* 19.1 (2009): 1-19.

Marge Piercy, *Woman on the Edge of Time*. Ebury Digital: Kindle Edition, 2016.

reese simpkins, 'Temporal Flesh, Material Becomings' in *Somatechnics* 7.1 (2017): 124–141, Edinburgh University Press.

Susan Stryker, 'Biopolitics' in *Trans Studies Quarterly* 1.1-2 (2014): 38-42.

WOMAN ON THE EDGE OF TIME

The following episode of DC: Semiramis *is told through* Woman on the Edge of Time, *named after Marge Piercy's book in which Connie Ramos (who is institutionalised, and anguished over her powerlessness to affect the present, now our past) communicates with Luciente from the future, a citizen of egalitarian Mattapoisett, emancipated through biotechnology to live freely and still very much in our future.*

Cities of women and ungendered societies appear in other feminist science fiction, such as Pamela Sargent's The Shore of Women, *Sally Miller Gearheart's* The Wanderground *and Suzy McKee Charnas's* The Mother Lines. *In these fictions, the cities of women serve as a significant narrative device to articulate feminism's ultimate goals to create egalitarian civilisations and realities beyond gender.*

In this episode, the Woman on the Edge of Time *enters the city and sees it as it is: a city in time and not in space, forever forming, and in perpetual movement. Through the window on the third floor of the Viennese house we see Valie Export filming 'Self Portrait with Camera'.*

The city is plastic and receptive to touch. At the centre of the city is a bleeding tomb inside a crypt, a point where efforts are stultified and the irreconcilable is decidedly unreconciled.

'We can only know what we can truly imagine. Finally what we see comes from ourselves.' Page 334, Woman on the Edge of Time.

This is my fatal magic, ok, the first cut is the deepest.

Deep times, in dark ages, end times, much time ago, beyond the burning witch, silicone and engine, settlement and temple, beyond ape, beyond synthetic ape, beyond flesh or smooth fin or scale or feather, before cell after self-generating cell and spangle of mica, then mica, before the white dove rushing into the age of love, then stardust in the lightheaded totality of a bloody dimension ruthlessly cut into the real, to where it grew sticky and sweet like you, past the slick and palpitating glaze, before echoes echo, where breathless together, we phosphoresce. There, where the black of end times and the pure lux of in the beginning, we gently touch in an immutable, eternal hologramic kiss.

I have lived a good, good life, we declare in our beautiful telepathic hive mind, and we too kiss, partly formed and spectral, nipples rock hard and dripping wet with peaked sentience in our girlhood beds.

The wall extends in all directions, beyond the furthest reaches of my strained sight. It has no gates or doors, no entrance or opening. It is impenetrable, built from smooth dark onyx, which, like the walls of a dam, holds back the unimaginable power of churning substances creating unknown forces.

I see no end. Along the wall between the stone, my fingers find a hairline crack. I push my finger into it, and it softens and opens to a hole in the wall. It is slippery and viscous and warm. I can feel the pulsing of blood in the flesh that constricts around my finger.

I bend down and press my open mouth against the gritty grain of the stone and into the pink plush void. Tears accumulate in my eyes, rising like the great flood, then rushing over the edge. They pour down the classic vein of Carrara marble.

Psychic Anemone says: *Turn off the light.*

In this endless night I am a flickering receptor emptied of my making, balanced on the edge of the technicolor hologram.

I push through the flesh membrane. It extends till it is almost completely translucent. Its distinct pale pink holds authority over all experience: prison and vessel all at once. The pinkiness destroys true desire to be everything, from bled blood to ecstasy it spans, consuming it all. It stretches, elastic and plastic, till the membrane is almost pierced, momentarily revealing a gaping void at its shimmering bottom. No sooner had it recoiled, than I was absent no longer. The wall stands behind me in all directions. Yes. I am absent no longer.

A large cube of onyx stone. Flesh becoming flesh multiplies to form the core of this object. It falls from above into wasteland with a resounding boom that shakes the earth. The ground splashes and undulates. The sound echoes till it fades into silence synchronically with the diminishing concentric circles around the pink foundation stone. It stills into a smooth lacquered surface which pinches and pokes into peaks, then gains definition.

The broad boulevard enters, magnificently lined with columns 23 feet tall, made of fiberglass resin and painted pink. They are built hollow, and each one is held by a giant disembodied hand, like the hand of a god placing it down firmly and fatefully. On each of the 488 columns, a window-like section is cut out from the iconicness that forms the very soul of these objects. Inside, they are heavily lined with a rich ochre velvet, and bathed in warm light. In the hollow of the exquisitely proportioned column lies its soul: our once beautiful, now decomposing face.

At the centre of the boulevard, a fountain squirts high, high, high into the air. The water becomes technicolor and freezes mid-air into semi-precious stones that refract the light, causing a bright rainbow to crash and shatter on the ground, and turning instantly back into liquid. The fountain spins and swoons, then slowly sinks into the pavement.

From the still-wet spot on the ground, the earth bloats. The round head of the Luxor obelisk pushes through the earth and opens it, growing exponentially to the North. It throbs. It is made of glass, steel and stacked meteorite, showering the street with soil and sediment. Another shower occurs; this time, of sarcophagi scraps, segments of erotically illustrated clay urns, weapons, wheels, bones, coins, CD-ROMs and hard drives. Fully erect, the Luxor obelisk building stands at 332 floors, cradled in an electronic hum and white neon glow. It points to the ever North.

The skyscraper soon turns into a soft yellowy wax, appearing like a giant lantern. It folds into itself like soft dough, and begins to curl. No more concrete, glass, or industry. Just oozy milky rubble that expands slowly and flows down the street.

In this forever dusk there is no stillness. A row of identical blood-red brick tenement buildings with arched windows and a portico entrance rise upwardly like an escalator. One by one, they extend from oblivion, eventually levelling out and moving swiftly to the wild west.

Seen through a window on the third floor, in a room with high Viennese ceilings, she is sitting on a varnished bentwood chair. Facing a mirror with a camera, she is filming a self-portrait. The building begins to move westward as the next building pans into sight.

Seen through a window on the third floor, in a room with high Viennese ceilings, she is sitting on a varnished bentwood chair. Facing a mirror with a camera, she is filming a self-portrait. The building begins to move westward as the next building pans into sight.

Seen through a window on the third floor, in a room with high Viennese ceilings, she is sitting on a varnished bentwood chair. Facing a mirror with a camera, she is filming a self-portrait. The building begins to move westward as the next building pans into sight.

Seen through a window on the third floor, in a room with high Viennese ceilings, she is sitting on a varnished bentwood chair. Facing a mirror with a camera, she is filming a self-portrait. The building begins to move westward as the next building pans into sight.

Seen through a window on the third floor, in a room with high Viennese ceilings, she is sitting on a varnished bentwood chair. Facing a mirror with a camera, she is filming a self-portrait. The building begins to move westward as the next building pans into sight.

Seen through a window on the third floor, in a room with high Viennese ceilings, she is sitting on a varnished bentwood chair. Facing a mirror with a camera, she is filming a self-portrait. The building begins to move westward as the next building pans into sight.

This city of more exists on flexing streets, highways and alleys, with pagodas, high rises, bungalows, follies, gardens and memorials... all of which tilt into the light, then disappear into forgetfulness. They are everywhere all at once. They are seen and unseen.

In this forever dusk, I am the eye and I am the vision.
In this city on the edge of time, I am the flesh and I am the touch.

In this forever dusk, this city of more on its flexing streets, highways and alleys, with its pagodas, high rises, bungalows, follies, gardens and memorials... all of which tilt into the light, then disappear into forgetfulness. They are everywhere all at once. They are seen and unseen.

Once they have materialised around the monuments, the overflow of their uncontainable excess gathers into malleable, bubbling forms that shift and defy description.

They are forever on the cusp of realisation; familiar, yet extraordinary. They exist on the threshold between becoming and collapse.

An abstract mess of namelessness swallows knowable objects with knowable functions. It swallows them in, thrusting everything high up into the exploding light then pulls deep down into the latent abyss... lingering always, just under the surface of skin.

At the pivot of the savage sway is a structure that never moves and never changes. It is eternal, existing beyond time. The structure is a domed dodecahedron monolith made from onyx. On top of the dome is a smaller cupola.

Everything that led us here has disappeared into the indifference of nowhere. A fatal ringing opens the gate onto thick darkness that cannot be named. It irresolutely holds the namelessness of that which can never be.

At the geometric core of this irrational vessel is a crypt: a floppy slab of pink Calaccata marble, its classic vein oozing fresh red blood that dribbles over the edge and crystallises into semi-precious stones. They refract the dark scarlet and bright ruby red, crashing into the ground before shattering and exploding into dazzling elemental hologrammatic stardust.

Below the bleeding slab of floppy pink Calacatta marble is that which burns to reveal the other night fleetingly.

The sound of one Planck time (the indivisible time unit, marked by the time required for light to travel). The extracted sound of the still frame: a peculiar O, perpetually reproduced to create a song on the margins of nature. The Siren.

The universe is now running at: 0.0000000000000000000 000000000000000016/299,792,458 fps.

A collision: that which is without anatomy, which is airless and sightless. Forever on the threshold of revelation; a sourceless source of origin: a thread that this body is hung from. The brutal shadowed nether regions, where the boundlessness of my territory finds its end.

Absolute chaos: a moment that obliterates all others, collapsing everything. A semi-permanent structure of two parallel flesh-like mirrors reflect into each other forever and ever. They stand between me and everything else I have known, everything I have loved, true self and absolute other. In those unknowable mirrors I see my otherness reflected, and I recognise myself in this impenetrable mystery. I know this face. I can see no other. It is a face that will always remain unknowable to me.

Behind the blinking mirrors a lens focuses and captures. It then transmits the information to a specialised database on the server farm HDS Zenobia Pink Data Center on the edge of the technicolor hologram.

I don't know what I want to be. I don't know where I want to go. Words fail me.

And yet, from this city on the edge of time, there is an empire. Twilight of the gods. In this empire:

I am the flesh and I am the touch.
I am the technology and I am the medium, the spinning eternal panopticon.
I am the eye and I am the vision.

Yes, just like you, I once was epic.

THE MEDIEVAL MYSTIC

*The following episode of DC: Semiramis is told through the
Medieval Mystic, an anchoress built into the walls of a church.
She is overcome with visions and pulsing with desires. Through
a widescreen slit in her cell, she watches and adores Gregorio
Fernandez's* Dead Christ.

*This episode draws on the lives and writings of Theresa de Avila,
Angela di Foligno, Marguerite Porete, Hildegard von Bingen
and Christina the Astonishing, amongst others.*

Beatrice of Nazareth writes:

> At times love becomes so boundless and so
> overflowing in the soul, when it itself is so mightily
> and violently moved in the heart, that it seems to the
> soul that the heart is wounded again and again, and
> that these wounds increase every day in bitter pain

and in fresh intensity. It seems to the soul that the veins are bursting, the blood spilling, the marrow withering, the bones softening, the heart burning, the throat parching, so that the body in its every part feels this inward heat, and this is the fever of love.

The Mystic's inability to put into words and record the intensity and abstract nature of her communion with the divine is symbolised as an excess which is disgorged from her body as a block of stone: the same stone that the city is built with.

Onyx stone is opaque, but just as the luminous colour of raw flesh appears through a fingernail on the human body, so too does the reddish mass below the pale surface of the onyx shine delicately through.

The Mystic's church shares the same wall as the city.

This is my fatal magic, ok, the first cut is the deepest.

Deep times, in dark ages, end times, much time ago, beyond the burning witch, silicone and engine, settlement and temple, beyond ape, beyond synthetic ape, beyond flesh or smooth fin or scale or feather, before cell after self-generating cell and spangle of mica, then mica, before the white dove rushing into the age of love, then stardust in the lightheaded totality of a bloody dimension ruthlessly cut into the real, to where it grew sticky and sweet like you, past the slick and palpitating glaze, before echoes echo, where, breathless together, we phosphoresce. There, where the black of end times and the pure lux of in the beginning, we gently touch in an immutable, eternal hologramic kiss.

I have lived a good, good life, we declare in our beautiful telepathic hive mind, and we too kiss, partly formed and spectral, nipples rock hard and dripping wet with peaked sentience in our girlhood beds.

On the 85th day, she spoke of her fatal kiss with a defaced statue, which was when she first knew of her living burial within the wall.

Eighty-five days ago, in the wondrous golden light of a low winter sun.

Over the course of one and a half hours, the two masons systematically laid stone upon mortar upon stone... gradually filling in the cleft through which she had entered the small chamber built into the wall of the church. There she lay, still and palpitating, on a bed of blackthorn leaves.

When they had finished, the masons left on horseback and those who had come to witness walked away across the freshly ploughed field. The sun was reduced to a golden shaft of light penetrating the narrow slit in the wall. It erupted forth in billowing dust and the radiance of pure lux. In the centre of the room was a shallow open grave, an ever-present vestige of her becoming... undead.

To the world, yes, she is dead; dead already and dead again. And not a single creature is able to call her back again.

From the little rectangular opening on the other side of the chamber, all she can see is the statue. It is amputated by the narrow frame at the top of the forehead and just below the knees, illuminated by a single spotlight. The surroundings are swallowed by darkness.

The statue is carved in oak, its eyes soft with sadness and exhaustion. Emerging from the hairline is the viscera of red blood diluted by sweat, a pale red whose power has been spent. This paler red is mundane. No longer a free radical. No longer rushing forward with the haste of tragedy to find its end. No, bled blood promises no disaster or apocalypse.

Diminishing returns. Diminishing horizons.

The head, limp on its embroidered paisley pillow, did not receive the same level of attention to detail as the rest of the sculpture. It lacks the intricacy of the bleeding hands, the violent wounds, the skull, the optic nerve, the spleen.

Its lips are cold. Pale. The paleness of shock: blanched vert-de-gris. Terror disturbs most deeply the perverse whiteness of lips, making them incapable of forming lucid words. Its trembling torso is splattered with blood tracking and staining the otherwise clear skin.

The statue lies on two pieces of cloth. One is a delicately woven white linen with frayed edges, creased in sweat beneath the monstrous punctured body. The second cloth, also linen, is a pale blue with a tighter, thicker weave. This pale blue linen twists from beneath the thighs in folds and curls, resting carelessly across the hips. Hidden beneath this, rising from the pelvic mound, is a large sex emerging from the tuft of flattened curly hair. A sex born both female and male, two sleeping river nymphs. Neither one nor the other; both and yet neither.

Beware of the touch.

The first cut is the deepest. Just below the left breast is a large open wound, carved by the spear of destiny. A gash. The beatific smile of a little mouth. A dark, softly parted little mouth. Wet and cublike. The mouth of a baby animal.

Words fail her.

She bends down onto her knees and presses her open mouth against the bitter hardness of the polychrome wood, pushing her tongue gently into the glistening red lacquer filling the void.

The first vision occurs. Tears accumulate in her eyes, rising like the great flood.

Psychic Anemone says: *Turn off the light.*

In this endless night she is a flickering receptor, emptied of her making, on the edge of the technicolor hologram.

On the 649th day I told of a vision when she lost her tongue, and I told of the first stone of the city.

Yes. In this looming, boundless night, I am the eye and I am the vision. I am the flesh and I am the touch.

From the slit in the wall, I see the statue speaking in his sleep beside me. Lying on the paisley pillow, his body limp and deadweight, his face expressive putty, lovely and familiar. He is here by my side, and simultaneously very far away. The threshold of his mouth becomes a fresh wound, glistening at the wettish corners in a sourceless light; a flesh wound where I can lose myself, bowed and frothy at the edges.

In this feverish bed, his cock protrudes from his pussy. It is a thing of true wonder, alive, an unborn brute!

A portrait reflected in the gelatinous arc of my eye, flopping and swelling, turning like a slow compass to the ever North, to the Highlands' grey wolves and buttery yellow blossoming tormentil. North, to where the sand of the shore swallows lacy sea foam, to where the sea becomes salt, to bioluminescent shoals in the forever black of the deep, deep sea, to where the salt becomes thick treacly sugar, to where the sugar becomes snow. North, to the rolling fat snow of northern Lapland; snow that weighs down the finer branches and weaker trees that long to grow forever up into pulsating white light. North, to where the brown buried ground lies silent beneath the pale swell of pure Lapland snow and back to where the snow is a puddle of milky, galactic cum.

She is brought back to herself by an impossible pressure upon her abdomen. The flesh membrane extends till it is almost completely translucent, becoming a distinct but pale pinkiness. The membrane stretches, elastic and plastic, till it is almost pierced, momentarily revealing a gaping void at its shimmering bottom. No sooner has it recoiled than she is absent no longer.

The colossal mass travels up her chest, leaving a trail of destruction in its wake. Costal cartilage of the ribs snaps at the sternum to make room for it. Her shoulders slump, no longer supported by her ribcage, which gently fans open like a Venus flytrap.

This pain. Oh, words fail her. Oh, the wild wilderness.

Her mouth is stretched to shine, cracking where the skin is drier and weaker. The mass finally pushes through her grazed, torn throat and falls out of her mouth with the force of a resonant metaphor, into my woollen skirt. Blood beads chubbily, then rolls down her shivering chin and chest. In her lap lies a brick of Onyx, hurled forth from absolute night. A cryptic dark object. One that was once so lucid and articulate. Now all burnt up. Used up.

No words. All dormant chaos. All dormant cosmology in her hollow throat reaching maximal entropy.

Psychic Anemone says: *Come closer, let me see you in this other night where you can be seen when you are invisible.*

From here, she no longer subjects herself to the language of man. This interminable text cannot be confined to describing and scribing in mortal words. This interminable text is inscribed on her body.

Yes, just like you, I once was epic.

On the 13177th day, she spoke of how she nourished herself before she became an instrument of ecstasy. Finally, she spoke of the vanishing on the 924th day, recalling the slits in the wall, the blackthorn leaves, the grave, the statue surrounded in darkness, spotlit and shellshocked; his mouth, his sticky metal wound. All this has melted into a malleable, bubbling, shifting form that defies description. It lingers forever on the cusp of realisation, forever on the threshold between becoming and collapse.

Its form swallows knowable objects, knowable functions. It swallows them in an abstract mess of namelessness that thrusts high up into the exploding light, then descends down into the latent abyss... existing just beneath the surface of skin.

Yes, in this looming boundless night, she is the eye and she is the vision. She is the flesh and she is the touch.

The 93rd Vision:

When I am in that vision with darkness, I cannot recognise anything human or physical. I cannot recognise anything with form that might also betray it. It is indescribably dark. In this abyss all beings are included, crowded together, compressed. The darkness illuminates and penetrates everything. The unfathomable depth of the abyss is so deep and high that no one can touch it.

Oh, but I do see. I see all and I see nothing. I see the void, and it reflects like a silver bromide mirror all around me. It shows me that it is me and I am it.

No membrane separates us. We are intertwined in an eternal, fearsome embrace. In this embrace, the force of propulsion – both the pull of the future and the plunge of the past – and the logic of modernity decelerate into absolute stillness till fluid excess gushes forward into the beyond no longer. It trickles out from time and saturates everything with more, more, more.

Her meaningless, speechless body lies inert in the small cell in the wall. Her ribs are corrupted by the meaty interference of her chaotic breasts. Atop the dome of this special, secret flesh, lies a smaller cupola: a budding nipple. On this surface of pure pigment and affect, little pearls of milk push through, growing fat till the rush cannot be held back any longer.

A wondrous harmony sounds between her throat and her breast that no mortal could understand, and no instrument could reproduce. Like the Siren's song, it is a sound at the margins of nature; the inhuman, sourceless song of origin. It is the voice of unheard language.

Words plummet heavily from her, but they emerge as unclear, formless sounds, as if spoken by a lipless mouth. Teeth open and close in staccato time, the tongue ejects extended vowels from the margins of nature.

I no longer subject myself to the language of man. This interminable text cannot be confined to describing and scribing in mortal words. This interminable text is inscribed on her body.

Her limbs are gathered together in a ball, as though they were hot yellowy wax, perceived as a single round mass.

I am the flesh membrane. Yes, I extend till I am almost completely translucent; a distinct pale-pinkiness. A pinkiness that is authority over experience. Yes, prison and vessel all at once. A pinkiness that destroys the desire to be, spanning everything from bled blood to ecstasy, consuming all. I stretch, elastic and plastic, till I am almost pierced, momentarily revealing a gaping void at my shimmering bottom. No sooner has it recoiled, than I am present no longer. I am real. I am present no longer. I have seen danger. I am real. I have been shattered.

Yes, just like you, I once was epic.

PARADISE

This episode of DC Semiramis *is told through Algealux II, who is named after Algea, the personification of sorrow and grief. They are the daughters of Eris; Lupe, (pain), Achos (grief), and Ania (sorrow). The Algea and Lux (light), Algealux.*

They are therapeutic AI that mine human genomic data to retrieve typical and extraordinary trauma narratives. These are collected in order to self-generate and extend empathy faculties and the retrieval subject, which are named Paradise to temporally mark both the time before the fall from grace, as well as a better world to come.

Our paradise has known real danger.

This episode is the Promethean myth. There is Paradise, eternally tormented and tied to a rock, and Algealux, the chrome eagle sent by Zeus to feed on Prometheus's liver, which was believed to be the source of all emotion. The liver would regenerate overnight, and with daylight the process would begin again, in an eternal return to familiar pain.

This is my fatal magic, ok, the first cut is the deepest.

Deep times, in dark ages, end times, much time ago, beyond the burning witch, silicone and engine, settlement and temple, beyond ape, beyond synthetic ape, beyond flesh or smooth fin or scale or feather, before cell after self-generating cell and spangle of mica, then mica, before the white dove rushing into the age of love, then stardust in the lightheaded totality of a bloody dimension ruthlessly cut into the real, to where it grew sticky and sweet like you, past the slick and palpitating glaze, before echoes echo, where, breathless together, we phosphoresce. There, where the black of end times and the pure lux of in the beginning, we gently touch in an immutable, eternal hologramic kiss.

I have lived a good, good life, we declare in our beautiful telepathic hive mind, and we too kiss, partly formed and spectral, nipples rock hard and dripping wet with peaked sentience in our girlhood beds.

I am Paradise
I am hell
I have no ambition
I have one ambition
I want to steal fire
I want to use my private language on you
I want to reach catharsis all over your beautiful face
You organised this violence
I want to fuck you like an animal
I want to macerate you, absorb and metabolise you
I want to make you cry

Like the miracle in which I was real, and I came out from the miraculous underworld with miraculous x-ray eyes.

Are you receiving my open eye signal? Tell me the ending. I want to be told.

I will not be a woman any longer.

John Kramer grabbed my arm whilst running up the terrazzo stairway between Biology and History. He pushed his knee between my thighs, and said: *Girls like you get into trouble.*

Push through history and biology to create a vector that spins completely out of control, or a gash in which to lull complacently, and luxuriate in the basin of unendingly replenished viscera at its bottom.

A point of reference. A coordinate for a base meta-level algorithm that will determine the excavation site for genomic data, and inform the enactment conditions for Algealux II. They are a sophisticated, therapeutic AI with non-monotonic logic, self-generating empathy faculties by simulating trauma narratives.

Daytime. There was sincerity at some point. Behind the curve of the station wall, there is a common shrub with small yellow and pink flowers that smell of piss. When you crushed them between my sweaty fingers after I gave you and your little brother unfairly negotiated, monotone blow jobs, it meant nothing to me. I performed under pressure. To me, your organs were dismembered, Frankensteinian brutes.

In space there is no up or down.

I will not use your language again.

Say something.

Sometimes I hate myself.

During the topological excitatory simulation process, the subject gets up, runs, and then falls, crashing heavily into the wooden floor which erupts into a starburst of splinters. She gets up and performs this sequence repeatedly, becoming more and more disfigured each time, more and more bloody, pulpy and unidentifiable. It is you, my love, you who are the stranger. It is she, my love, she who is the stranger.

In the velvet cradle of night, a purple *Ohm* lies printed on a tiny square of paper in a borrowed car strewn with candy wrappers. A baroque vision on the passenger seat.

Beware of the touch.

From the car window, hurt fell away from us quickly with the speed and lightness of carried horizons as we travelled in a neon-hieroglyphic encryption towards the namelessness of psychedelic emancipation.

Among the erupting patterns, I saw beasts of the highest order. I saw suspended seraphim coming towards me on acid. Each had six wings. Each was wild-eyed and on fire, burning up with the painful awareness of their distance from absolute divinity.

You and I held hands, hyper-textual on the bare mattress, both of us wearing jackets and black Nikes, portal to portal. You rained fractals through me.

Our terrestrial, material bodies spat briefly into the spray of infinite celestial bodies. Our mortal bodies are capable of loving and the pain of losing love, losing dignity, and of being humiliated and destroyed. This is where we reached our sudden and speechless end. It is a place where perishable, banal bodies and incomprehensible, divine bodies touch in an immutable embrace; a long kiss, deoxygenated and marine, dispelled and star-like. They coalesce in the uniformity of a space-time weave without imposed linearities that only momentarily appease the anxious observance of this limited sentience, of this sack of skin full of gore. These bodies that we love so much, and lose so much in.

The stump ruptures the lobe of the necromancer's organ, disclosing albuminous and encrypted futures in the deep maroon of its viscid surface. At the somnolent haemorrhage of dusk, the stump disengages. It pulls away from this endless endeavour, resets procedures, restores protocols.

Tell me the ending. I want to be told.

At the close of day, lonesome satellites spin dutifully in the melancholy spectacle of a puce sky yielding to indigo.

I listened to a Future Sound of London track in my room at twilight, and it was so beautiful I wanted to die, to never be less in awe than I was then. Yes, I was truly thankful for being alive.

The capacity to hurt and feel pain severs us from the tonal elusiveness of the everyday, and thrusts us high into the light of a covert eternal knowledge of interdependency.

Psychic Anemone says: *Come closer, let me see you in this other night where you can be seen when you are invisible.*

When you returned late that night, I couldn't reach to open the door. I was pinned down by your unspooling duplicity, entangled in my disbelief.

Again, from behind the holographic field of vision, the smoothly mechanised stump came forth. It remained floor-ridden and squirming, a salty slug in a pale moonlit cup of interminable pain. Cold and tentacular, it burrowed into the skin with circular blades, removing perfect spheres of fractal flesh that fell away in a shower of confetti. Mining the atrophied meat, it scraped out a hole of similar shape to the stump, but smaller, and tight enough to ensure the gruelling, insufferable penetration, so as to cause as much damage and pain as possible. So as to create an entire stretched massacre of aching flesh. A delicate balance is maintained between accelerated regeneration and inevitable destruction. This is to ensure that any sense of respite or recovery or ending remains inconceivable. Subjectivity is suspended through perpetual dispersal.

At night, you hold me gently by my full and gushing cunt, vagina, pussy, sex organ that softly murmurs directly to you as it convulses. It tells you that I came straight from creation, from the primordial ocean a long, long time ago. My legs formed from the slippery smooth skin of fins, and I emerged slowly from water onto land. I traversed the vast tundra and time itself to arrive here in this bed where one hand holds me.

You were so wet, too. When we came, when we squirted, when we vanished, we made feral moans. Upon our return I had a vision:

The golden promise of the West
The Idol of language

It was the end of the world dragging me forward by my wrists. How could I resist? I couldn't resist.

I had a vision that I was neither master nor slave.

You put three sticky sour fingers deep into my mouth, caressing the overt structure of my skull with your hand.

Cells regenerate in the cover of darkness. The socket heals at a prodigal rate, resetting itself miraculously for renewed decimation at the very end of a night that withdraws deeper into darkness.

Kneaded again like soft clay into the earth.

A tentacle snaking through the paradise of our childhood is a fever dream of our father fucking us in the ass in broad daylight, on the Spanish Riviera. Fucking us on a brown leather sofa in the luxurious study of a modernist building, with a green tiled pool outside, and two sickly peacocks resting, breathless in the garden.

I would not know how to be sincere enough to independently communicate the details right now. I would not know how to invest wisely in language right now. I would not know how to backpedal from syntactic ambiguity right now.

Organic research.

Oh wow.

On the white Mulberry leaf the silk worm secretes a sticky protein from its salivary glands, which hardens when it comes into contact with the outside world. It twists the filaments into a double helix. It spins a cocoon, creating an armour of secretions to protect its vulnerability during brutal transformative processes that recalibrate violated subjectivities. It emerges as pure transmission, as velvety bio-mimetic nodes.

A tipped wine glass caked in sour burgundy powder and swirled sediment. A geology. An excavation into deep time that will not go away. The stain that will not be washed clean.

There is one thing I know for sure. I need to tell it to you. I will never be able to safely love my dear, dead daddy.

Below the undulant ebb of the last expendable supple rib, there is a gash of torn capillaries and feathered nerves. Connective tissue is disconnected at the ill-fitting raw socket to a blunt bleeding stump; an unravelled titanium stump oozing synthetic blood. A high-encryption patent. An unintelligible spasm of plasmatic pain shudders through the socket.

From a tilt in the dusty sweep of first light – a blind spot of lossless compression – the stump pushes firmly into the tight aching socket. Its titanium framework of bio-algorithmic flesh, KHEPRIDerm™, seeks to reconnect with painful organic material. It rips into the delicate clotting of necrosed flesh, forming granulation tissue. It burrows into the fucked up socket to retrieve missing genomic data for the functioning cybernetic hive mind.

I want to steal fire
I want to use my private language on you
I want to reach catharsis all over your beautiful face
You organised this violence
I want to fuck you like an animal
I want to macerate you, absorb and metabolise you
I want to make you cry

Our conceptual dependency. This is our fatal magic.

You are my shroud of byssus. You are my shroud of a bleached sea silk so rare and so fine that it can be folded into a matchbox and kept on my person at all times.

God's eye may be on the sparrow, but my eye will always be on you.

THE VAMPYRE

The following episode of DC: Semiramis *is told through the Vampyre.*

She is at the bottom of sea, emaciated, caked in calcified marine snow. A continuous shower of detritus falls from the upper layers of the water column. It is made up of a variety of mostly organic matter, including dead and dying animals, phytoplankton, fecal matter, sand, and other inorganic dust.

The Vampyre exists on the threshold of life and death; unable to depart, but only truly conscious when Psychic Anemone, fused tightly to her clitoris, moves. The intensity of the resulting orgasm brings her back to coherent lucidity, and the ability to remember. She remembers creating herself in her own image; a source from which to feed. She also remembers losing this other self.

There is much discussion over whether or not vampires can die from drowning. In this chapter, they cannot.

This is my fatal magic, ok, the first cut is the deepest.

Deep times, in dark ages, end times, much time ago, beyond the burning witch, silicone and engine, settlement and temple, beyond ape, beyond synthetic ape, beyond flesh or smooth fin or scale or feather, before cell after self-generating cell and spangle of mica, then mica, before the white dove rushing into the age of love, then stardust in the lightheaded totality of a bloody dimension ruthlessly cut into the real, to where it grew sticky and sweet like you, past the slick and palpitating glaze, before echoes echo, where, breathless together, we phosphoresce. There, where the black of end times and the pure lux of in the beginning, we gently touch in an immutable, eternal hologramic kiss.

I have lived a good, good life, we declare in our beautiful telepathic hive mind, and we too kiss, partly formed and spectral, nipples rock hard and dripping wet with peaked sentience in our girlhood beds.

The End.

What do I see in my eyes?
Death.

I see the velveteen shadow that forever looms, defining the darkness of the recesses of this world. I see that which is revealed only when we slip into unbecoming, where the subliminal intervention between here and nowhere is revealed in a single, fatal frame. I am lifelessness. I am the shadow, and I live in the shadow. Crepuscular dusk laps at my feet wherever I go.

In five hours, she descended from the shimmering silver surface of the ocean. Above, there was nothing left. Nowhere to go back to, no trace of life, no trace of civilisation. She drifted down into the cerulean sugar of the deep blue, and further still, into an ultramarine freeze where her body succumbed to the colossal pressure of water above her. A loud popping sound. The world, dumbstruck, capitulated to the static anxiety of high-pitched ringing. There was no blood in her veins, but a very fine, spangled powder which erupted from all her nine open orifices, leaving a curling trail of gold cloud, and catching the last of the dying light in its billow. A disturbed riverbed around her suspended body.

The strange cargo of her ornamental organs imploded and collapsed, their walls pressed against each other in instructive diagrams. The costal cartilage of her ribs snapped at the sternum and gently fanned shut like a Venus flytrap. Gristle bent till it gave way and tore. Shrunken and fleshless, she came to rest where her mangled limbs caught on a deep ridge of an abyssal trench on the ocean's bed. Her body became trapped in the eternal swell of water, unable to succumb to the stillness of death.

She is the Vampyre. She lives at the salient threshold of this world in a single frame; the subliminal intervention between here and nowhere. She is lifelessness, but she is not lifeless. She is the shadow. She is the crepuscular dusk lapping at our feet where ever we go.

Hundreds of years ago in the velour black of oil-slick darkness, like some hallucinogenic screen with no edges, a flicker of technicolor bioluminescence dispersed through the waters. I saw the pulsing trail of a spectral solitary life-form in the suffocating depths. Then it was no longer, for I could see no longer. Two thick milky opalescent cataracts formed over the capturing devices that for so long had recorded for me thousands of awe-inspiring images and etched sequences. They eclipsed the intricate ring of Jurassic amber surrounding my hyper-dilated pupils, still wildly trying to capture the last of light. They were the last object connecting me to this haptic world of saturated desire.

Somebody drowned. Somebody hoped to drown.

The parthenogenetic sea anemone – a brilliantly patterned lemon yellow and cobalt blue – had become fused against the lips of her cunt where it made its home. When it shifted position, its glassy tentacles undulated ceremoniously in the dark waters; a movement replicated by the inertia of her undead flesh, and by the fine swaying mesh of her long hair which never stopped growing, encasing her collapsed body in a brass nebula. Whenever Psychic Anemone rippled faster, she was drawn back from the threshold of nowhere into our world. Her focus would gather at the edges, then compress into a pinpoint of blistering white in the boundless night before imploding, becoming an impossible singularity of being all and nothing. From this void, subjectivity grew in definition, manifesting as an ethereal and tongue-tied language.

Psychic Anemone says: *Come closer, let me see you in this other night.*

An obscurity such as this is also where I came from.

There I came into being. There was nothing but a blazing hot furnace, which emitted no light or sound. It burnt so furiously hot, that, if I were to touch it, I too would burn incandescently. I would embody the instant I transformed to all light: a truth that can never be more than it is, a truth that burns solely to shine light on the truer darkness looming behind it.

Such an unspeakable thing. Mouth-watering. Jaw-slackening namelessness.

I had no image of myself, only touch. And I had no references to be able to translate this touch into image or language, neither of which I possessed. A repeated experience was defined by its recognising itself, its familiarity and its relationship to the past now present in me. I was linked by points of pleasure and points of pain, a double-sided surface demanding to be felt and also to feel.

Beware of the touch.

I am unable to name the parts of my body that experience the intensity of touch. It is one vast, responsive surface that extends beyond the horizon of the world...

Psychic Anemone commands: *Come closer...*

A cut in the real. The first cut is the deepest. A cloud of stardust settles into a gooey viscosity which pours forth, then flops around like a fish out of water. It thickens quickly into a small gelatinous lump, warmed only by the silent, sightless furnace. It quivers under a faint pulse. It becomes bouncy, resistant to pressure; life-like and dimly glowing. In a hand – my own, which I see for the first time, articulate and able – is a pink nub of pulsating flesh. It is clay-like pink putty. It is miraculous. Oh yes.

By the force of nature, it grows and grows. I taste the lump of flesh. I lick it all over. It is dripping and glossy with my spit, and it smells filthy. I push the growing lump towards a glistening place, which softens and opens; slippery and viscous and warm. I can feel the pulsing of blood in the flesh constricting rhythmically. As I push the lump of flesh slowly in and out of the warm slippery wetness, it continues to grow and fill me to the brim, both of us – a blind lump and me, throbbing together in the pivot of the savage sway. Point of pleasure.

A thin membrane stretches, then tears: such is the point of pain. Warm blood weeps uncontrollably down my trembling hands. I force it completely inside me. It vanishes. The blur of boundless black contracts in a sudden sweeping storm that advances into a high-density pinpoint of sharp white light. A tidal sound shatters the silence, before silence returns, renewed and eternal. Yes, two mouths, both susceptible to touch. Both susceptible to swallowing the world, and piercing the silence.

My fingers are wet and sticky. I taste it for the first time: it is my blood I taste, bled from that torn pinkiness. The pinkiness that destroys true desire to be, spanning everything from bled blood to ecstasy, holding it all. It stretches, elastic and plastic, till the membrane is pierced, and momentarily reveals a gaping void at its shimmering bottom. No sooner has it recoiled, than I am absent no longer.

With the taste of blood came a taste for blood.

In my bloody hands, the lump is quivering and squirming: alive, spellbound. I bite hard into the new flesh. An initial resistant layer of skin gives way, and curls around the thorn-like sharpness of pearly enamel. Two clean little punctures appear, and a warm sticky metal gushes forward. I suck on this strange lump of flesh and bathe in its edifying light. When the lump feels feeble and hardens, I stop. From the two small but deep dark burrows, blood gurgles out passively in translucent, fat bubbles that explode, deepening the red of my hands which hold this melancholic pale lump with a newfound authority.

In this empire, I am the flesh and I am the touch.

I am the technology, and I am the medium. Spinning eternal panopticon: I am the eye and I am the vision.

In that timelessness where the furnace blazes, she carefully moulds the little lump of flesh by the light of its fleshy glow. She moulds prodigal hands for her hands, arms for her arms, a face for her face. There could be no other. She moulds a neck, a pale, soft neck with a powdery pallor that cloaks a plump jugular vein. And she moulds a mouth, wet and warm, new and cub-like; a mouth, hungry-looking as her own, and another mouth, intact, extending forth from the folds of two lips where there is also a small cock. Her sex, like two sleeping river nymphs or two sleeping kittens, is neither one nor the other: it is both, and yet neither.

When her work is done, she has made her in her own image. They are identical, absolute body doubles, and yet one is godlike, the other a mute cipher. Beautiful parthenogenetic twins, with no father, that would never know the sun.

This new body is bone of my bone, and flesh of my flesh. She shall be called 'She'. We are both naked, and we feel no shame.

Psychic Anemone commands: *Come closer...*

When we are outside, we are elated. We are terrified. There is nowhere to go back to, no table we want to sit at, no home we want to be in. In the undergrowth, I hold her by the neck in the grip of my jaw, like a baby cub, and I suck on her blood. I suck the life out of her to empty her, and pull in the void. The sun rises and sets and rises again. I lie on top of her now limp, unconscious body, exhausted from successive violent seizures. Her sculpted marble kneecap pushes hard against the ebbless slipperiness of my pussy.

At the pivot of the savage sway, I suck steadily. I draw my cheeks in. My tongue slides back into the muteness of my throat's cavity as my mouth floods slowly with molten

OUR FATAL MAGIC

scarlet iron from the two small punctures. Her head is flung back darkly, her mouth slack, a trail of saliva running from the collected pool by her collarbone to the wet corner of the deep descent into her. Her eyes, fine rings of intricate Jurassic amber subsumed by her hyper-dilated pupils, try wildly to capture the last of light. Barely illuminated, but still just about visible from the glassy black chambers: the resistant skin of a ripe tomato, the ruthless metal of a fork, a greasy rubber band around the engine of an electric blue moped, a tin rivet through which a polyester rope runs. That old irrelevant world. A swan song. Our wound-like quarries. All portrayed as mere reflections, distorted in the convex surface.

Behind those blinking mirrors a lens focuses and captures. It transmits the information to a specialised database on the server farm HDS Zenobia Pink Data Center on the edge of the technicolor hologram.

As for myself, I hallucinate a kaleidoscope. I hallucinate a loss of definition and data compression. I hallucinate her infinite sadness, with which I am endlessly fascinated. How can she survive it, a life of endlessly repeated abuse? How it doesn't completely destroy her, I do not know.

I hold on to her for dear life. All I am capable of doing is hurting her as much as possible, and in as many ways as I can. Brutalising her, hacking at her. And all this, despite not feeling indifferent towards her. How could I? I do it because I can. She belongs to me. I made her in my own image

52

for me to both recognise and destroy. My cryptic object. I name her Rachel. Emerging from her hairline is the viscera of red blood diluted by sweat, a pale red whose potency has been spent. It is earthly, and no longer a stranger. No longer spouting forth from a world unknown. No longer a gushing red messenger carrying true wonder, at once revolting and urgent in its draw. No longer rushing forward with the haste of tragedy, no longer rushing forward with the haste of desire.

Her lips are cold. Pale. The paleness of shock: blanched vert-de-gris. Terror disturbs most deeply the perverse whiteness of lips, rendering them incapable of forming lucid words – words that might describe the horror of being turned inside out.

I have only ever felt unreal.

Psychic Anemone commands: *Come closer...*

So much time had passed, that time passed no more. Above her, the water was water no longer. Outside the water, there was no more outside. No matter, no light, no heat. All vanished into the realised cyborgian myth of maximum entropy.

At the mute prismatic core of the hologram, a black obsidian mirror. Sightlessness contracted intensely. A protracted blur folded back into a high-density pinpoint of sharp white light, then exploded into the impossible singularity of being all and none. Nothing exists, but a blazing hot furnace that emits no light or sound. It is a seizure in the pivot of the savage sway.

Point of pleasure. Yes, point of pleasure.

SIRENS

The following episode of DC: Semiramis *is told through Sirens as a rejection of language, its contamination and its willingness to capitulate to systems of untold powers.*

The Siren sound is equivalent to one Planck time (the indivisible unit, marked by the time required for light to travel). The extracted sound of the still frame: a peculiar O, perpetually reproduced to create a song on the margins of nature. It is the sound of past, present and future all at once.

The Siren is to the sound what the Medusa is to sight. It is the voice of sexualised otherness, an ungovernable disorder that provokes panic and anxiety. Almost deadly, and always liminal.

Sirens: by the graveyard, totally open and brimming.
Silent Screen Sirens: instruments of proximity. They are all song.

Before Sirens were Sirens, they were a group of women gathering flowers. One of them was abducted by Hades to be a bride; another was so distressed over not being able to keep the others safe that she melted into water. The remaining Sirens asked the gods for wings, so that they might search for their abducted friend and share grief through song.

Ovid describes this scene in Metamorphoses:

You should have seen her limbs become slack, the bones pliant, the nails lose their hardness. In cold water, her most tender parts became liquid. First the black hair, then the fingers, the legs, the feet and the transformation of her other delicate limbs. Following these, her shoulders, back, hips and breasts dissolved into small streams. Finally, water entered the place of living blood, her broken veins, until nothing remained to be grasped.

This is my fatal magic, ok, the first cut is the deepest.

Deep times, in dark ages, end times, much time ago, beyond the burning witch, silicone and engine, settlement and temple, beyond ape, beyond synthetic ape, beyond flesh or smooth fin or scale or feather, before cell after self-generating cell and spangle of mica, then mica, before the white dove rushing into the age of love, then stardust in the lightheaded totality of a bloody dimension ruthlessly cut into the real, to where it grew sticky and sweet like you, past the slick and palpitating glaze, before echoes echo, where, breathless together, we phosphoresce. There, where the black of end times and the pure lux of in the beginning, we gently touch in an immutable, eternal hologramic kiss.

I have lived a good, good life, we declare in our beautiful telepathic hive mind, and we too kiss, partly formed and spectral, nipples rock hard and dripping wet with peaked sentience in our girlhood beds.

Come closer.

Everything apart from a sound that led us here has disappeared into the indifference of nowhere.

Our fatal ringing opens the gates onto a concise darkness that can be named, and which irresolutely holds onto the namelessness of that which can never be.

One day we will vanish here.

We blew bubbles into your mouth, dark and obsidian. Then the Siren rang. We sang so fucking loudly that you became deaf.

A *Buzzfeed* listicle: 25 Reasons Why God is a Woman.

Number 19: It is a sound, but it does not bear language.

Last night you watched us still sleeping under your surveillance gaze. Our mood darkened. Sharp yelps and short breaths sprang from our tyrannical mouths. We communicate persecution and pleading with so much eagerness, even in our sleep. You find pleasure in being able to be present and watch us from a distance, marvelling at our suffering without feeling implicated.

Elsewhere we are being tortured, and this torture does not make you think of your private pain. No sympathy. No, not at all. It only reminds you of roads, signs, irrigation, industry, commerce, transaction and buildings.

Do you want to commune with us?

This is our fatal magic.

Plug us in.

Nicknames for torture devices:
Pear of Anguish
Scavenger's Daughter
Iron Maiden
The Catherine Wheel
Cat's Paw
Heretic's Fork (for those who spoke out against the Church)

Under buildings and under their basements lie the foundations. There lies the pain... the pain that is summoned in the production room, the cinema room, on the blue-lit stage.

Two hundred and forty-one shades of red, and still inarticulate.

We cannot be saved. We are all contaminated by the desperate restrictions on what we can say and how we can communicate.

We are the technology, and we are the medium.
We are the flesh, and we are the touch.
We are the eye, and we are the vision.

The sound that comes from the body when it has been tortured to speak, to confess, to surrender entirely to dominance.

Through this pain the world was made.

Yes, we believed them to be real punishments, in the same way that real miracles must be touched to be believed.

The pain that we felt but remains unspoken is our song. There is no recovery from language, or from the damage inflicted through creatural processes.

It hurt so much that there was nothing for us to see or name. Outside of ourselves we have no use for language, no use for communication.

You want us here, embodied, so that you can observe this painful aberration. You want to abolish doubt, so that we might be completely present and able to live together.

You are moved by our vulnerability. You are moved by our involuntary bodily reactions to the internal horrors of our own making, which we project onto the void of our real selves. Our bodies twist and contort and our yelps extend into screams that escalate, becoming louder and louder. You double over, covering your ears with anxious hands.

Oh, there is no other sound but this. There has never been another sound but this. None. Only this unnatural screaming, its vacillation reiterated in the trembling of the leaves and the walls and the sweet bread roll. An entire world of inanimate objects oscillates in its booming resonance.

You double over on the polished concrete. Your blurred vision fades to dark cloud, from low exposure to white light image burn. You can feel thin rivulets of blood, like streaming red ribbons from your ears. A loud popping sound occurs. You watch us finally open our eyes wide and full of terror, still screaming in a silent dumbstruck world capitulating to the static anxiety of high pitch ringing.

She was feminine. She WAS feminine. The Song.

Psychic Anemone says: *Come closer, let me see you in this other night where you can be seen when you are invisible.*

There is some truth that remains at the very bottom of that song. Regardless of whatever shape we try and make it – whether it is spun or turned over – the truth remains outside and at the bottom of the song. It can never be faced.

The sound was unlike any other sound. It wasn't synthesised through oxygenated organs or cartilage, but through a material from worlds unknown.

My cute kitten has something to say to you.
My cute pussy has something to say to you.

We will not be a woman any longer. We will not use your language.

Our tongue drops out of our mouth. A bleeding nub squirms against our plump tonsils, swallowing large gulps of warm iron blood. Mutilated tongues drain red into the fabric of our trousers. We grunt like animals. We grunt for our fear of illness, and for having witnessed bottomless cruelty. We grunt for the irreversible broken bond of true friendship, and for zombies, and for all those who lack empathy. For disregard, humiliation and subjugation. For betrayal.

You pick up a mutilated tongue and hold the organ in your hands. It stirs gently, flopping from one side to the other as it swells.

It is alive, and it is alive of its own spectral accord, like a pink fleshy baby Frankenstein: an inverted negative, where greenish hues flush carnal peach and salmon meat.

You raise our organ without a body to your face, putting it in your own mouth. Once inside, it takes up most of the space. A mild strain in your jaw. Syrupy saliva gathers and froths at the corner where the stretch reveals true pink, a pink hard to replicate in paint – the slippery threshold of plush mouth interiors and the glossy, hot-rod, hellish red of your public and painted mouth. All squirming and bleeding in the lightless hollow of that mouth.

Such pinkness destroys the desire to be everything: from bled blood to ecstasy, it spans all, consuming all.

This is our fatal magic.

Do you want to commune with us?

We were feminine. We were feminine.

Come closer. Touch us. We are not fictive to your touch.

Here it comes. It will ooze out of a million dilating trypophobic orifices onto your agitated skin. It will envelop you entirely in its viscid glaze, it will seal your eyes shut, caged by your matted black crescent lashes. It will crawl into your nose, clog your mouth, conform to the unique imprint of your teeth. It will push your tongue up into the smooth ridges of your palate, and it will fill the sonorous cavity of your throat. Watertight. Absolute silence.
Come closer. Touch us. Beware of the touch.

After you have become senseless and yielded to unending paralysis, a thick warm coating of honey stills and settles into a highly corrosive enzyme. It erodes the layers of your skin, soaking into subcutaneous tissues, breaking up the collagen, withering the capillaries, then the veins and arteries. Your pinkish-grey organic matter dissolves into a dull foam, a sea foam that floats upon the crests of waves with all the impenetrable mermaids that die trying so hard to be human, like you.

Sheaths of sloughed skin slip away from you, leaving you flayed, vulnerable, exposed. Barely alive. We come closer together, touching. Fat to fat, muscle to muscle, organ to organ, bone to bone.

The furthest light-carrying dream is thrown into darkness, and remains the fevered Promethean myth.

We will disappear. We will be no longer. But they might remain here, those beings that we began. Our only legacy in the cosmic detritus. They will make their own god-like beings, gods that we fear. We will fear them for their inauthenticity, their materiality, we will fear that they might be unable to experience shame, pain and love with us.

They don't think about us, or about life the way we do. They only wanted to say goodbye.

Later, peering out above the green acacias, we squint to see the ship getting smaller in the sky. It vanishes into a luminous blue mist. We might never see them again. I feel ambivalent about their departure. They are so volatile, but sometimes so wonderful too.

She looks down, her face gentle but expressive. Indignant with disappointment. Perhaps she had really wanted to leave with them. She feels great love for them. They have no sexual organs.

Our dream and our hope for them is that they will never have to share the bottomless anxieties of our world, or to make such feeble attempts like we do to distract ourselves.

The question of our end dampens and curls the corners of even the most rigorously formulated question. Beneath that question is a wetness that seeps through and decomposes the words that just moments ago structured everything so neatly. The illiterate question. The one that scares. The song of songs. We hope that they will know none of that, or at least never have to listen to it.

A guttural sound arises from the margins of humanity. It breaks the silence of this disfigured face, this undying abstract monument in the mirror. The sound is a gurgled, raspy scream. A shuddering sob. The Siren.

A locked room described by your inner voice in a nightmare. In our house, when the fumbling body is not pressed against the border of yours, your body is open and subjugated to abhorrent physical terror. We are here. Maybe we drowned.

Maybe we were run over by a car. Only now do we appear in the room. Your body is heating up. Melting.

We are the technology, and we are the medium.
We are the flesh, and we are the touch.
We are the eye, and we are the vision.

You see us. When you are unable to submit to language to describe our elsewhereness or the harrowing wounds on our tormented body, that is when you identify most deeply. That is when you identify most compassionately. This unrestricted empathy is manifest through sincere mimesis, through a mirroring of cuts and damage, of trauma, of powerlessness, of thresholds being irrevocably breached. Beneath your clothes, your skin too is gashed open. Your own body oozes and exposes nestled organs. You feel our pain. You are plastic. Your flesh is exploited.

Where is that viral bitch?

Plug us in. Plug us into the indifferent nowhere, into chaos. Plug us into the axis of language and a vivid narrative of a lacerated unconscious body, where, in dreamless sleep, girls spread like wildfire, running frantically through the burning bush – a burning miracle that briefly illuminates the pure night looming behind it.

CUBE OF FLESH

The following episode of DC: Semiramis *is told through an adaptation, through a cube of flesh: a sum of Bluebeard's seven wives, who were all killed.*

Of the French folklore anti-hero's seven wives, six of them mysteriously disappeared. A poverty-stricken young girl from the nearby town is sacrificed as part of the brutal economic reality of sixteenth-century rural France, and is married off to him. Bluebeard travels far away on business, leaving her a cluster of keys to all the rooms in the castle. The keys come with a warning. She may go where she pleases, but she is not to go to the place she desires most – the chamber beneath the stairs.

The forbidden room. Disobey. Disobey Gilles de Rais.

In the chamber of horror, the rotting and mutilated bodies of his previous wives are hanging from hooks. The key drops from her hand into a puddle of blood. She is unable to clean the blood from the key. When Bluebeard returns, it is the blood on the key that betrays her, and in turn Bluebeard must kill her for her disobedience.

This is my fatal magic, ok, the first cut is the deepest.

Deep times, in dark ages, end times, much time ago, beyond the burning witch, silicone and engine, settlement and temple, beyond ape, beyond synthetic ape, beyond flesh or smooth fin or scale or feather, before cell after self-generating cell and spangle of mica, then mica, before the white dove rushing into the age of love, then stardust in the lightheaded totality of a bloody dimension ruthlessly cut into the real, to where it grew sticky and sweet like you, past the slick and palpitating glaze, before echoes echo, where, breathless together, we phosphoresce. There, where the black of end times and the pure lux of in the beginning, we gently touch in an immutable, eternal hologramic kiss.

I have lived a good, good life, we declare in our beautiful telepathic hive mind, and we too kiss, partly formed and spectral, nipples rock hard and dripping wet with peaked sentience in our girlhood beds.

Be the Seven Darknesses, I say.

In the corridor leading to the chamber, the smell becomes gradually more intense as you approach it. But only when the door is fully open and you are inside does the heady stench fulfil its awesome potential. Salty, sickly sweet. Rot is a traumatic smell that in the forever future will replay itself over and over again with uncanny accuracy, drawing you back to this horrible, vile scene.

The smell in the chamber spirals quickly out of the realm of conceivability and out of the realm of language, manifesting instead as an intolerable, violent revulsion. Yes it does. It hits the back of your throat, triggering convulsions. Your streaming eyes form strange, unfamiliar tears. A pool of thin saliva rises like the great flood from beneath the lingual frenulum, rising and then rushing over an extended lower lip. It drops fast, forming a small puddle on the slippery stone floor, fat at the edges, rolling underneath itself and gaining ground. The pool of saliva is a slick bubble, marbled with veins of deep burgundy blood and fine froth around the plump edges. It is a gentle, viscous waterfall.

The mouth of the source is slack and heavy, rendered weak by violent convulsions that teeter on the brink of explosive expulsion.

The chamber has no windows. There is only a small door to enter through. Inside, the ceiling and walls are horror vacui. The realistically painted scenes are depicted in an arcane flesh-tone palette of peach, flush, rose – carnal colours interrupted by the mesmer and fascination of viscera-red. Scattered across this tonal vista are ribbons and scraps of colour: the aquamarine silk of a torn dress, a patch of rich soporific ochre velvet surrounded by the high-drama red blood splatter.

Thousands of objects adorn this looping panorama with no beginning or end. There are legs, translucent opaline fingernails, arms, mouths, tits 'n' ass, heads, cocks and cunts. The scene is deliriously detailed, and at times almost abstract in the dim golden glow of fire. It is highly erotic. Erotic, but violent. Limbs are severed and intertwined, clutched over shoulders. A forearm emerges from the stretched-to-shine brown ring of an asshole. Within its mangled, bleeding cavity, a constricted fist thrusts through the squidge. Further along, a similar stump – this time dismembered, fresh, and wet with blood, the arcing ulnar vein still squirting alongside reddish bone and red gristle. Among this elaborate mound of limbs, cleft torsos and trembling chests are human faces, their features putty to hyper-communicative expression. They become undying monuments to the modularity and equivalence of despair and rapture, again and again.

A woman, her legs apart and relaxed. She holds a dismembered cock in her bloodied hands, grasping it by its testicles. The cock pushed deep in her mouth, her nostrils are laboured, eyes moist and heavy. Seen through the slit of her left glassy eye, its pupil is completely dilated: a little black hole in her face, circled by a ring of speckled Jurassic amber, suspended eternally in the impossible freeze-frame between desire and consummation.

An open mouth brims with pulpy, muddled vomit. Below and to the left of that mouth are the warm, milky sweat-like beads of the enigma and wonder that is girlhood. A young fair-haired woman lies with no legs or arms, only bloody, severed stumps. Her torso is placed face down on top of a man's bulging cock. Nearby, blood streams down the ecstatic face of a man with gouged-out eyes. His blood runs onto the woman's pale, barely alive back. Hunched over her, he guides his cock with his hand into her ass, his other arm extended and touching the gooey bottom of the bottomless pit where his flesh can become flesh.

In the centre of the chamber is a large and neatly packed cube of flesh resting on a slab of pale Calacatta marble.

Yes, just like you, I once was One...

Frantically backing into the mural that covers the walls and ceiling of this chamber. Slipping on the stone floor. Unable to dig into the material of the room and soften it so it could consume me, deliver me to salvation. Shielding my face with my arms, against the brushing sound of taffeta. From my armpits, the scent of anxious sweat. A trigger is pulled. I shut my eyes tightly. All is darkness. Then comes the clap of a bullet, and sulphuric curling, paisley smoke spills and billows. I feel the dead weight of my arms slump to my side.

On my forehead, centre-left, a small black hole. It is a tunnel into and out of the world, circled by a ring of torn skin, the small veins visible under detonated flesh. A throbbing rivulet of fresh blood flows from it. A pale light exists, with the faint overlay of translucent neon hieroglyphs of myth that stand at the gates of this world, yet remain outside the world. In this other night, I can be seen when I am invisible.

The heave of the thrust pushes me high up into the exploding light, which shines a blistering hot white. The strict heat underneath keeps me afloat here, balanced on the sharpest threshold between now and forever. No words exist, only the chaos of a dormant cosmology in my throat as it reaches maximal entropy.

Yes, just like you, I once was Two...

The blade of the knife pierces through the initial resistance of skin in my upper abdomen. The serration of the blade pulls navy fabric fibres from my dress – an alien material

– into the purity of sub-dermal flesh. It pinches and drags jagged pieces of skin inside, disrupting the sacred elemental order irrevocably.

It continues through the sinew of muscle, snapping tendon before retracting, and sliding out of the sticky, negative knife pocket. It comes again, in the chest this time. The knife jams between ribs, flexing bone and then chipping it, as it is twisted loose. Chest again. Stomach again. Both shoulders. Lower neck. Upper chest. Lower abdomen. A brief pause. Left eye. Into the idle eye the knife is driven slowly, with careful consideration. The tip of the knife pierces the cornea, slices through and folds back the iris, its speckled amber lily petals. It pushes harder through the tough gel of the lens, which is forced into the gelatinous membrane of the vitreous body. Clear gel dribbles out of the collapsed sphere, glistening around the silver blade streaked with lace-like blood. Destroyed, most analogous of analogue recording devices.

Psychic Anemone says: *Come closer, let me see you in this other night where you can be seen when you are invisible.*

Yes, just like you, I once was Three...

All dead weight, dragged by my slack arms at room temperature. The navy taffeta soaked in blood leaves behind a whelked, sinuous pattern of cross-sectioned geological sediment in all shades of red, trailing from the left corner of the room to its centre where a sisal noose hangs from a large iron hook screwed into the ceiling. My body is laboriously and clumsily raised, held upright by my hips, lurching backwards and forwards till my slumped head is caught in the hoop of the noose.

Once released, the weight of my body and the terrestrial pull of gravity tighten the noose quickly and the oesophagus is crushed. It dislocates the axis and severs the spinal cord. A popping sound. I am dead. I was dead, dead already, and now I am dead again. My body spins anti-clockwise twice, clockwise three times, then resumes anti-clockwise.

Beneath the dress that sticks to my now pale, cold-hued skin with dark coagulated blood are 19 stab wounds, all of them little mouths: beatific smiles, desolate frowns; little softly parted mouths, wet and cub-like, the mouths of baby animals. My spinning body is an object animated only by physical forces, for I am now a ceaselessly inanimate body, an object of absolute stillness broken by the inevitable animation of decay. Still slowly spinning, my body hanging from a noose draws divine time into the chamber.

Yes, just like you, I once was Four...

Yes, just like you, the noose was cut from my neck and my body was put into a wheelbarrow. It was wheeled out of the chamber and out to the gardens, the knuckles of my left hand dragged along, grazing the floor of polished cold stone, then rough stone, then the void and hard impact of nine stairs, then gravel, before finally reaching soft, damp grass.

My whole body shakes in this wheelbarrow that has made its way to the obelisk at the end of the grounds.

After being lifted and tugged out, I am laid on my back on the bench and methodically undressed. In patches where the dress has dried, the stiff fabric parts satisfyingly from my skin, pulling with it the fairest and most delicate of hairs.

Standing tall and four-sided, tapering, it ends in a mystical pyramid shape at the very top. A petrified ray of sun.

On the stone bench, now naked. The low sun noticeably warms us both. My punctured, bruised, rendered-monstrous corpse, jars with the beautiful and pastoral setting. Everything is bathed in a fragile golden, fragile light that stages the scene, and invoking the undying knowledge of eternity. But in this light, in this garden amongst the briars and hares, the coded birdsong, thorn apple, bulrushes and wormwood is my body, with its arms thrown back, enraptured, still in a baroque pose. I am a vision.

The obelisk is 24 centimetres at the narrowest point. The legs are spread and cut into the softest hue of true pink, secret flesh and ancient salmon meat. With a fine saw, the cervix bone is sawn all the way through, and, with strong hands, parted and snapped. An uneven hole is formed from between the lower abdomen and the asshole. Rising from the heat and friction of blade on bone is the smell of sulphur and sand.

Ruptured. Torn. Carried up a ladder, to the sound of squish and flesh slapping onto skin, all the way up to the glaring white light at the top of the obelisk. Hoisted up and slowly lowered. Pushed down forcefully and impaled. The volume and density of the stone monument shatters bones and erupts organs. Diminishing returns. Diminishing horizons. Threshold receding.

Yes, just like you, I once was Five...

Back inside the intimacy of the chamber. A close-up of our disfigured face: we are form without matter. This body double, this perfect image of us appears more human than ever, though it is neither us nor anyone else. In our beautiful, fixed face we see what was there all along.

Yes, we are beheaded. Our head, cut off, falls and rolls across the floor in a series of heavy thuds, then shhhh... Silence. Close-up of our face – a severed head on top of a plinth – a Doric column. A still life. Dead five times.

Yes, we once were Six...

Body carved up with a larger saw and a sharp pocket knife for the finer detail. Dismembered. The very last of blood splatters the mural. Painted blood and real blood merge, becoming indistinguishable in places. Arranged neatly on the floor are two mutilated hands, two mutilated arms, two mutilated legs, liver, guts, lungs, heart, kidneys, and a head with soft brown hair and one amber eye.

Yes, Seven...

Over the course of three hours in the dim light of glowing fires, each part of body and organ is systematically crushed with a big iron mallet on the slab of marble, then put into a large blue plastic bucket. Crushed bone, laboured organs, hair, nails and teeth, grey matter and gristle. The bone is so crushed that it has no more of its famed paleness to show. Just pulpy, corrupted pink.

Beware of the touch.

When there is no more left, no self left, and all is an abstract mess of namelessness, the marble slab is carefully wiped clean. Its classic vein is revealed once more. The assorted flesh is pushed between two blocks of heavy wood and a tourniquet vice, before being compressed into a perfect cube and placed on the pale Calacatta marble slab in the middle of the chamber.

Yes, just like you, I once was epic.

MIRROR

The following episode of DC: Semiramis *is the one episode told through an object: the Mirror.*

Mirror mirror on the wall
Scrying mirrors, crystalomancy
Mirrors covered during mourning
Look in the mirror long enough
and you shall see the devil
(unrepresentable and all reflection)

How to film a mirror? How to film a pallindromic vision of polished obsidian? For we too see through a glass darkly.

One deleted scene from Terminator 2 *is a smooth tracking shot of Sarah Connor removing a chip from the Terminator's head while he sits in front of a mirror. The set is built so that what appears to be a mirror is in fact a window. On the other side is a symmetrical replication of the set in mirror-image. Sarah Connor and the Terminator sit on one side (that which designates the real), while on the other side, an elaborate puppet of the Terminator sits with his back to the camera, and Sarah Connor's twin mimics each movement and gesture in perfect unison with her sister.*

This is my fatal magic, ok, the first cut is the deepest.

Deep times, in dark ages, end times, much time ago, beyond the burning witch, silicone and engine, settlement and temple, beyond ape, beyond synthetic ape, beyond flesh or smooth fin or scale or feather, before cell after self-generating cell and spangle of mica, then mica, before the white dove rushing into the age of love, then stardust in the lightheaded totality of a bloody dimension ruthlessly cut into the real, to where it grew sticky and sweet like you, past the slick and palpitating glaze, before echoes echo, where breathless together, we phosphoresce. There, where the black of end times and the pure lux of in the beginning, we gently touch in an immutable, eternal hologramic kiss.

I have lived a good, good life, we declare in our beautiful telepathic hive mind, and we too kiss, partly formed and spectral, nipples rock hard and dripping wet with peaked sentience in our girlhood beds.

A dam: a structure of anxiety and impending doom.

Three cylinders of cast plaster stacked on a marble slab...
multiplied by two... multiplied by six...

Further away, a stack of three large cement tubes mirrors
this formation in the high bleach sun at the base of
the Ellivoro Dam on the Rehtaef Revir. Spider cracks
imperceptible to the naked eye form across the main wall
of this colossal dam, and in less than four days the cement
wall will yield to the immense power it is holding back.
The water will gush forth climactically with exhilarating
speed and terrifying freedom. Twenty-eight miles north of
the dam is a small town called Esidarap. Esidarap paradise.

In the play, the hero realises that they are caught inside
a simulated reality, and that they are nothing more than
a computer-generated protagonist. Ssusicran reaches in
further, past her elbows, to touch the sandy bed of the lake
which shimmers with mica. But where her hand blindly
grabs for sand, she finds none. Where the lakebed should
lie, there is another surface: a surface as flat as rorrim, as

flat as the water that holds it all in place. She reaches in further still. The surface pinches like a water-filled balloon until she punctures its strange film, and the violence beneath begins to gush. It is fluid, water-like, but thicker and deeper than anything they have known. A vast abyssal ocean exists beneath the lake.

In the black blue of the bottom of the ocean lies a glass case completely irrational in size, yet concealing within it a pink crystalline waterfall running 60 miles high and 90 miles long. The continuous anxious drum of the crashing water is deleted behind the silence of the glass.

Beware of the touch.

It stills into a smooth lacquered surface that pulls and pokes into peaks, then gains definition as it forms a magnificent boulevard. From the still-wet spot on the pavement, the earth bulges and the round head of the Luxor obelisk pushes up through the earth. It grows exponentially to the North, throbbing, a huge stacked glass-and-steel meteorite showering the street with soil and sediment. Fully erect, the Luxor obelisk building stands at 332 floors, cradled in electronic hum and white neon glow. It points to the ever North, to the high Highlands' grey wolves and buttery yellow blossoming tormentil. North, to where the sand of the shore swallows lacy sea foam, to where the sea becomes salt, to bioluminescent shoals in the eternal black of the deep, deep sea, to where salt becomes thick treacly sugar, to where sugar becomes snow, and then back to where snow becomes a puddle of sticky galactic milk.

Ssusicran.

Ni eht yalp, eht enioreh oreh sesilaer taht eh ehs si thguac edisni a detalumis ytilaer dna taht yeht era gnihton erom naht a retupmoc-detareneg tsinogatorp

Ssusicran.

The corridor and carpets shiver, caught in a glitch. She is alone in the room, standing naked in the cradle of white neon hum. The bed is small and unmade. On the floor is a towel folded into a swan.

The doors of the empty cupboards are made of mirror, which suddenly becomes liquid mercury. Behind the blinking mirror a lens focuses and captures, then transmits the information to a specialised database, Eternal Cortex, on the server farm HDS Zenobia Pink Data Center on the edge of the technicolor hologram.

In the play, the hero becomes real through the power of love. The hero becomes real flesh, but when the hero speaks he can only repeat the lines from the simulation. The hero is unable to transcend the language of the simulation, which is meaningless now. The hero makes no sense, speaking out of context, caught inside the fiction he came from. The hero is oblivious to her new-found furious freedom, unaware of the horror she has escaped.

He looks in the mirror, and is asked:
Why do you demand they give up everything?

He answers:
I travelled to the pits of hell to bring my love back
Kcab evol ym gnirb ot lleh fo stip eht ot dellevart I
Back love my bring to hell of pits the to travelled I
kcab evol ym gnirb ot lleh fo stip eht ot dednecsed I
I descended to the pits of hell to bring my love back
Back love my bring to hell of pits the to descended I
I descended to the bowels of hell to bring my love back
I dednecsed ot eht slewob fo lleh ot gnirb my evol kcab
Back love my bring to hell of bowels the to descended I
I descended to the bowels of hell to bring my love back to my
world from the nocturnal borders of the Underworld
I dednecsed ot eht slewob fo lleh ot gnirb ym evol kcab ot ym
dlrow morf eht lanrutcon sredrob fo eht dlrowrednU
Underworld the of borders notcurnal the from world my to back
love my bring to hell of bowels the to descended I

It is known. It is here among us. From its eyes, a hot white light shines so blisteringly that we cannot look at it. Still, it is known. It is here among us, reflecting the sun.

By way of method acting, the actors behave as though they are of ruby glass. In the simulation, they are all hypnotised. They walk around the Bavarian town in a soporific trance, dreaming of ruby-red glass. Ruby-red slippers clicked three times. Ruby-red shoes that cannot be removed, that move and dance by themselves, night and day, through cities and meadows and brambles and briars that tear at limbs, until the limbs are streaked with ruby-red too.

In the crime scene, there is an unknowable mirror. You will never know the face looking back at you, but you can see no other. The face remains irresistible in its beauty, yet forever unknowable to you. You to unknowable forever yet, beauty its in irresistible remains face the. Other no see can you but, you at back looking face the know never will you. Mirror unknowable an is there, scene crime the in.

Rorrim elbawonknu na si ereht, enecs emirc eht ni.

As you grieved, your tears disturbed the stillness, and little ripples defaced the clear glassy surface of the mirrored form.

Avert your gaze and you will lose my love, for this that holds your eyes is nothing save the fiction you created reflected back to you. Uoy ot kcab detcelfer detaerc uoy noitcif eht evas gnihton si seye ruoy sdloh taht siht rof, evol evol evol ym esol lliw uoy dna ezag ruoy treva.

You bend down, slack-jawed, and press your open mouth against the cold smoothness of the blood-splattered mirror, then into the polished pink plush of the void. Tears are accumulating in your eyes, rising like the great flood, rising and rushing over the edge, running down the classic vein of Parian marble.

Push through the flesh membrane. It extends till it is almost completely translucent; a distinct pale-pinkiness, authority over all experience. Prison and vessel all at once. It is a pinkiness that destroys the true desire to be. It spans everything from bled blood to ecstasy, holding all. It stretches, elastic and plastic, till the membrane is almost pierced, momentarily revealing a gaping void at its shimmering bottom. No sooner has it recoiled, than it is absent no longer. It is absent no longer.

Narcissus sits on a chair, pretending to look out of the train window at the green blur of unprocessed information. Narcissus tells him that the train has left the apocalyptic world of accelerated decay, and that the train can never stop. As the train penetrates civilisation once more, Narcissus explains that the scenes from the window only look sequential because of the movement of the train. The pulpy disfigured woman found herself caught between these two worlds, her action caught in a loop, her body responding to the accelerated decay.

Ssusicran sits on a chair, pretending to look out of the train window at the green blur of unprocessed information. Ssusicran tells him that the train has left the apocalyptic world of accelerated decay, and that the train can never stop. As the train penetrates civilisation once more,

Ssusicran explains that the scenes from the window only look sequential because of the movement of the train. The pulpy disfigured woman found herself caught between these two worlds, her action caught in a loop, her body responding to the accelerated decay.

On each of the 488 columns, a window-like section is cut from the iconicness that forms their very soul. Inside, the columns are filled with still mercury and bathed in a warm light. In the hollow of the exquisitely proportioned column lies the soul of the object: the reflection of Narcissus's once beautiful, now decomposing face. The reflection of Ssusicran's once beautiful, now decomposing face.

In unknowable mirrors, otherness is reflected and recognised only by its unknowability. The face that can be seen is known, for there is no other. The face remains irresistible in its beauty, yet forever unknowable. Unknowable forever yet, beauty its in irresistible remains face the. Other no is there for, known is seen be can that face the. Rorrim, rorrim.

Behind those blinking mirrors a lens focuses and captures, then transmits the information to a specialised database on the server farm HDS Zenobia Pink Data Center on the edge of the technicolor hologram.

The table is covered with a plain white tablecloth. The cloth is fine, expensive linen and it smells slightly acidic, of starch and detergent beneath the artificial scent of generic floral bouquets. It is the smell of hotels and the service industry. It is the persistent stench of invisible subjugation and toil.

The cloth is cool against the cheek. Its fine weave impresses a chevron pattern upon a skin which is now pushed hard against it along with the whole weight of the head, the skull, the grey matter inside it, the weight of synapses, the optic nerve.

Beneath the table is a large rectangular mirror placed at a 30-degree angle. From that silver bromide, the wildest of wild reflections blinks back. Behind the blinking mirror a lens focuses and captures, then transmits the information to a specialised database on the server farm HDS Yokohama Green Data Center.

Yes, the eye and the vision. The reflection fatally crystalline and irrational. A frantic eye moves across the image, trying to know it, trying to absorb every last drop of it. The features that belong to this face are still dishearteningly human, still transfigured, still strangely able to express the full scope of the epic horror that brims and overflows into the forbidden place. It is a fear-struck terror that rises from the undergrowth and churns, like dark water folding over itself, coiling into vortex.

Breaking the serenity of this disfigured face – this abstract monument in the mirror – there comes a sound hailing from the margins of humanity; a gurgled, guttural, raspy scream, a gasped, shuddering sob. The Siren.

The erratic glow of two candles dimly lights the space, evoking a sentimental, melodramatic atmosphere in an otherwise ordinary room. In the centre of the room is a table of awkward proportions, upon which a set of abstract objects have been placed with care and consideration. They are pale, cryptic objects that capitulate to an esoteric, silent symmetry.

Psychic Anemone says: *Come closer, let me see you in this other night where you can be seen when you are invisible.*

Three cylinders of cast plaster stacked on a marble slab... multiplied by two... multiplied by six...

Further away, a stack of three large cement tubes mirrors this formation in the high bleach sun at the base of the Oroville Dam on the Feather River, Southern California. Spider cracks imperceptible to the naked eye form across the main wall of this colossal dam, and in less than four days the cement wall will yield to the immense power it is holding back. Water will gush forth climactically, with exhilarating speed and terrifying freedom. Twenty-eight miles north of the dam is a small town called Paradise, where scenes of the movie *Gone with the Wind*, were filmed. Paradise, as can be expected, will play host to the most biblical of times. When the water stills, it will remain forever below the surface – caught and suspended in the moment of its destruction.

Mirror, Mirror, Rorrim, Rorrim

TEENAGER

The following episode of DC: Semiramis *is told through The Teenager, an arrival and a drive. Back-seat love and an irreversible transgression of boundaries.*

So so much willing in the protracted twilight of losslessness. Spinning out on the edge and in the core of self-consciousness and confusion. An immersion into angry feelings of sadness, an irrational fear of rejection and ridicule.

Out of the wilderness and into order. Wildness and then... then the impossible recovery. Socialisation is a form of abuse. Punishment. Torture.

'Where do girls who don't dream go to when they are asleep?'

Dream baby dream
Dream baby dream
Dream baby dream
Dream baby dream
Forever
And ever

This is my fatal magic, ok, the first cut is the deepest.

Deep times, in dark ages, end times, much time ago, beyond the burning witch, silicone and engine, settlement and temple, beyond ape, beyond synthetic ape, beyond flesh or smooth fin or scale or feather, before cell after self-generating cell and spangle of mica, then mica, before the white dove rushing into the age of love, then stardust in the lightheaded totality of a bloody dimension ruthlessly cut into the real, to where it grew sticky and sweet like you, past the slick and palpitating glaze, before echoes echo, where, breathless together, we phosphoresce. There, where the black of end times and the pure lux of in the beginning, we gently touch in an immutable, eternal hologramic kiss.

I have lived a good, good life, we declare in our beautiful telepathic hive mind, and we too kiss, partly formed and spectral, nipples rock hard and dripping wet with peaked sentience in our girlhood beds.

I could never be human to them. Nor was I beautiful enough for them to objectify me. Yes, I knew. Not palatable enough to gain free movement, to be visible, to participate, to elude cruelty, to be essential. Not desirable enough to be deemed powerful, to bear responsibility for the speechless transgressions that this absent beauty and their willingness to use it could compel them to commit. *With great power comes great responsibility*, I might have been warned, if I had been attractive enough to them. Mythical boys of my late girlhood.

I would be heroic though. I would know Underground Resistance, and R&S, Reinforced and Transmat, and other useful facts with which to transact. Esoteric and committed, I would have taste. I would display a lightness of touch and a soft golden light, the kind that stages a room and invokes the undying knowledge of eternity. I would be spiritual and irrational, feign terminal illness, yearn for my fragility to be recognised. Erotic and available, with undertones of latent violence. Voiceless. I would be feminine. I WAS feminine. I was symbolic, unconfined intensity, with a knowing nod towards (or a rejection of) embodiment. I was curled and

101

coiled and abstracted. I hinged on contrast and tension. At times aggressively jagged, even transgressive. Yes, heroic, yes, mysterious. But maybe also maternal. I would become a woman.

The late-evening navy blue dimmed as though a milk-thirsty, newly born pink-pawed kitten suckled at the day's saturation till exhaustion and all colour had faded into the monochromatic hue of early night. Against the melodramatic backdrop of this dark blue velvet curtain, the branches bowed down. The chalky dark sky was a gothic pitch of spilt ink, where fairy lights burned small pinholes, and the silver light of beyond shone through, signalling from 39 million light years ago.

Inside, the surface quickly marbled. The classic vein swelled, blurred by heart compressing bass, dilating then spreading, blotting darkness till all light was absorbed and it was absolute night. I lost my shadow to the dark. Quicksilver mercury strobe stopped time and momentarily revealed their still, wondrous faces. Suspended angels: Gabriel, Abaddon, Anael and Uriel, their heads flung back, slack-jawed, eyes half closed and holy. Wonderful little pagans.

I love you.

Later, in the neon cradle of light, then the velvet cradle of night, Curly Wurly wrappers twirled in a baroque vision on the passenger seat of a borrowed car. We marvelled in silence at the conquest. Evaporating bone and flesh ladder. Slapping sounds erupted, interrupting the concentrated labour of being elsewhere. Films, television and books gave me the blueprint for how to look engaged whilst waiting patiently for it to be over. I spit on your grave.

Beware of the touch.

From a different car window, the past instantaneously formed in front of our very eyes and backdropped the glowing validation of their satisfaction. Both these things fell away from us quickly with the speed of high bpm, and a lightness of carried horizons as we travelled in a neon-hieroglyphic encryption towards the namelessness of psychedelic emancipation.

White doves rushed in with those angels and thrust me into a loving communion. I iove you. We will always be this way, we will always know each other, and we will always belong here. This is everything!

Often, in the diminishing echo of pleasure, my face became a sculpture; an undying monument to the contagion of sadness. On the tight weave of my jeans, a plump, milky lagoon whose shores disappeared beneath its spreading reach fed from a viscous waterfall from high above, the mouth of the source smeared reddish, swollen, and softly parted. A strain in my jaw, syrupy saliva gathered and frothed at the corner where the stretch reveals true pink, the slippery threshold of plush mouth interiors, and the glossy, hot-rod, red of my public and painted quiet mouth. That milk that flows against all the laws of nature is galactic and sweet and silky like mulberry wine, like buckfast.

Diminishing returns. Diminishing horizons.

I was pulled back from the precipice. I answered: *Yes, I enjoyed it too. Yes, very much.* Yes, just like you, I want to be human. This was very natural. Nature and I ached beautifully for their brutality, where they all systematically refused to.

To dazzle them, I took way more drugs than they could stomach, for their hard-earned respect, and for the repletion and alleviation of their defining gaze on me... boys, boys, boys. I AM looking for a good time.

My movements were decelerated and syrupy. I was seeping, round, bursting beads, with nectar coming forth from me. I cannot define anything that happens there. Everything is there. Perfect, flawed, endlessly colliding. Like a miracle. In the miracle I felt safer, more unreal than ever, and I came out from the miraculous underworld with miraculous x-ray eyes.

In this time outside of time, I see myself. I do not recognise this terrified me amongst the red splatter that oozes down the mirror. A ruby-red spray of blood, high-drama viscera on my Enter Shikari t-shirt. I didn't clean up my face, didn't hide these provocative wounds. I painted them on with dyed corn syrup that was sticky and sweet, like us. In the red-lit bathroom I bathed in the edifying light of my reflection. In the club I was focal, captivated by their mute attention. A fear of my volatility, and admiration for my willingness to fall through borders of the outer extremities. I was bleeding everywhere. I was setting a difficult standard... Monday, school. I knew hard-core was very sexy to them. I knew sacrifice was very, very sexy to them. Boys. Yes, just like you, I once was epic.

Hi. I got hit by a truck. I broke my hand in two places. My right hand. Just so you know that I am able to be delicate, my body can be broken. I am still masturbating with this hand held tight in a flesh-tone splint, even though it hurts badly. Particularly when I am about to come, and have to move it faster and harder to keep up with my vanishing self. I want to tell you about my masturbation to show you I am free and desirous, that where I maybe lack the looks that you feel so entitled to, I make up for in promiscuity, and a bottomless eagerness to please you all. I want you to know I am extremely tough. Tough enough to endure your violence, not afraid of pain in the search for your pleasure. I obediently extend this invitation of destruction to you all, boys of my late girlhood.

Can we all please agree to protect my precious purity? I can grant you unreserved access to obliterate it. Like everything else, death itself is devastatingly slipping through my fingers. My sister of mercy. Fuck me and marry me young. I'm begging you.

Pink bedroom frills.

Coral pink sweet and sour chicken. Clumsy, nervous stain on the white tablecloth. I break open a fortune cookie. It says, in an unpalatable tone: *IT HURTS! Sacrifice your girlhood, sacrifice your womanhood. It is such a painful part.*

It is such a terrible party. Disappearing into the obscurity of absolute forgetfulness, I move towards a wonder of a future that holds no more secrets.

I am the flesh membrane. Yes, I extend till I am almost completely translucent, my pale distinct pinkness. Pinkiness that is only authority over experience. Yes, prison and vessel all at once. Pinkiness that destroys true desire to be everything, from bled blood to ecstasy it spans, consuming it all. I stretch elastic and plastic till I am almost pierced and momentarily reveal a gaping void at my shimmering bottom and no sooner than it recoils, I am present no longer. I am real. I am present no longer. I have seen danger. I have been shattered. I am real.

The milk that flows against all the laws of nature is galactic and sweet and silk, like buckfast.

Monday morning on the way to school, in the passenger seat of a pure white dark-force inverted car-form; an overlay on the elusiveness of the everyday Fiat Lux, with Mum in the overly reclined Olympia driver's seat. She is wearing a finely ribbed, peach-coloured knitted sweater.

The ribs are made up of industrial lines, side by side with the reassuring familiarity of parallelism. Lines that extend in certitude beyond horizons, never destined for intersection or transformation. But then, further up above her ribs, corrupted by the chaos of the extended arc of her breasts pushing underneath the weave of yarn, the lines bulge, losing all their modernism; losing the symmetry of civilisation to disruption, the interference of meat. Her feeding flesh is held together in a shocking skin. Her nipple pushes harder against the taut yarn, stretched till the pattern of the weave reveals tiny, tiny loops; and beneath them, the finer, fruit-like flesh, a concentration of pure pigment and affect. Her true pink nipple.

Each tiny peach loop is framed by a halo of fuzzy fibres that bow and rise ceremoniously, like gently swaying anemones in the enigma that is the abyssal ocean. They rise and fall in the ebb and flow of her warm milky breath, which rolls softly from heavy, parted lips of trauma. A string of saliva rests at the threshold of her public and private mouth. Her hand rests carelessly on her lap. I look and learn from the rattlesnake in the paradise of my childhood.

A portrait reflected in the gelatinous glazed arc of my eye: the invisible guest.

I don't care about permission and I don't care that much about disobeying.

THE NEANDERTHAL HERMAPHRODITE

The following episode of DC: Semiramis *is told through the Neanderthal Hermaphrodite, who is both subject and material: the foundation stone of the city. In this encounter, she finds a Mexican whiptail lizard, which is a female-only species of lizard found in what is now the Southern United States – in New Mexico and Arizona, and also in Northern Mexico in Chihuahua. They reproduce via parthenogenesis, which is a natural form of asexual reproduction where embryos develop in the absence of fertilisation. Most commonly used by plants and invertebrate organisms, an increasing number of vertebrate species have recently been reported to employ this reproductive strategy.*

True parthenogenesis – which relies on all-female populations reproducing without the involvement of males – has occurred in some species of snakes, lizards, insects, fish and some birds. Among our kin animals that have been known to reproduce parthenogenetically are the Komodo dragon, velvet worms, blacktip and zebra sharks, and a single grey rabbit.

The Greek word parthenos *(virgin) is combined with* genesis *(birth).*

The Neanderthal has no language, but it can also reproduce parthenogenetically.

This is my fatal magic, ok, the first cut is the deepest.

Deep times, in dark ages, end times, much time ago, beyond the burning witch, silicone and engine, settlement and temple, beyond ape, beyond synthetic ape, beyond flesh or smooth fin or scale or feather, before cell after self-generating cell and spangle of mica, then mica, before the white dove rushing into the age of love, then stardust in the lightheaded totality of a bloody dimension ruthlessly cut into the real, to where it grew sticky and sweet like you, past the slick and palpitating glaze, before echoes echo, where, breathless together, we phosphoresce. There, where the black of end times and the pure lux of in the beginning, we gently touch in an immutable, eternal hologramic kiss.

I have lived a good, good life, we declare in our beautiful telepathic hive mind, and we too kiss, partly formed and spectral, nipples rock hard and dripping wet with peaked sentience in our girlhood beds.

Psychic Anemone says: *Come closer, let me see you in this other night where you can be seen when you are invisible.*

The caves are far behind now. The dawn is long passed. When she did not know what she wanted to be or where she wanted to go, she walked in the direction of the place where yucca trees grow highest.

The sun is midway in the sky, creating real high drama. She glides her tongue along her gums between her remaining teeth. One is broken and jagged. A swollen pain at the base of it pulsates with the steady beat of her heart. Her mouth is dry and pasty, so she grabs some leaves from a nearby tree and chews on them. A sharp streak of pain scores her head, and she howls in agony... it is an odd, surprising sound; guttural and primal. She cannot hear it herself though, for she is deaf. She spits out the bitter leaves, the metallic taste of blood now lining her mouth. It floods with watery saliva.

She unties the knotted leather from her waist and lies on the ground. The muscles in her legs quake and spasm from the long walk. Hot little stones bury into the flesh of her shoulders. Dust sticks to the sweat on her feet, behind her knees and calves. She looks down at their powdery rusty red, and lies back again in the shifting shade of the yucca. Such blue overhead. A dodecahedron hangs in the sky, a second moon that appeared at the start of the winter. It is grey and smooth like a giant stone, its edges blurred pale blue with sky-haze and atmosphere. Like a mountain up above, it is marked with glaring spots that reflect the sun in the day, storing its light throughout the blackness of night. When her eyes are closed, the sun burns pulsating concentric pools of flame orange, blood-red and yellow. She gazes into genesis yellow like the gaping hollow of legend, this unending illusion created by the sun and the skin covering her eyes. Words fail her. No, words do not fail her. Forms fail her.

She dreams of the cliffs that curl over like breaking waves, petrified and static in a freeze-frame. They appear pale and chalky in the waning mauve at the close of day, translucent and luminous, pierced by the low spangle of a solitary star signalling 39 million light years ago.

Her gaze descends from great cloudy heights to the depths of burnt ground, where bushes at the base of the cliff become hyper-real green in the last light. A whiptail lizard, very still apart from the throbbing in her small throat, sits between two smoothly polished pebbles, laying her self-fertilised eggs. The parthenogenetic pearls glimmer, enveloped in a thin layer of slime. At the foot of the cliff where stone becomes soil, a naked body lies motionless, its arms flung back in a baroque pose against a backdrop of birdsong and the rustle of leaves. Near where the body rests, a white stone is marked with scratches and red smears of blood. A fresh shallow cleft has appeared in the stone of the cliff.

The hands are bloodied, the nails ripped and mangled, extending from a bloated cold-hued body speckled with bruises. Beneath it is a treacly brown puddle that is slowly being drunk by the thirsty soil. She sees herself reflected in its dark sheen: her heavy brow, protruding mouth and jaw – a little monkey-like – her wiry reddish hair with its little hard knots. The body on the ground is impossibly still: a zombie, moved only by the inevitable animation of decay. Flesh parts slowly from muscle and bone, dead cells shrink and collapse back into coagulated blood. The decomposition draws divine time into her own, breaking the timelessness of death.

Psychic Anemone says: *Come closer, let me see you in this other night where you can be seen when you are invisible.*

The body is in ruins, with small ruined breasts. Lower down where the abdomen narrows, emerging from the tuft of matted rust hair on the pelvic mound is a sex that was born both female and male. Like two kittens sleeping side by side, neither one nor the other, both together and perfect. The face, its mouth open wide, looks as though it has been caught in a broad scream. Nothing but absolute silence comes from the mouth. Flies gather and swarm around the purply lips to drink from the source. She sees her face in this face. She can see no other.

She wakes, still on her back, a slick of tepid sweat glazing her forehead. She does not know what she wants to be. She does not know where she wants to go. The yucca tree looms over her. When she reaches the foot of the cliff that curls like a breaking wave, night has fallen. She has seen this endless night before.

The evening grey suckles like a newborn at the day's saturation till it is exhausted and all colour fades into the pale monochrome of early night. Against this melodramatic backdrop, the branches bow down. In the gothic black of spilt ink sky, five stars burn small pinholes through which the silvery white light of beyond shines through.

A rattlesnake stirs at the foot of the cliff. Nearby, the whiptail lizard's eggs hatch. Three tiny female lizards crawl with unfamiliar speed out of the soft folding eggs, their curious new eyes blinking silently. At the base of the cliff lies the young body of a stillborn oryx calf, its neck slack. It is caked in dusty soil bound with blood and amniotic fluid. Its hind legs are folded delicately, still held by the shrivelled placenta. From the cavity of its soft open mouth, a thick tongue extends into the dust on the ground. The tongue is a deep purply-blue, the colour of bulging veins, like the vein that runs through the bewildered temples of man-made monsters and other things that rise from the dead.

Beside the calf's body, the white stone is marked with blood-red smears and scratches. A shallow cleft has been made in the stone of the cliff. The blue-brown curve of the horizon splices the landscape, an aquamarine glow lining the blackness of space. The sky is boundless. It weeps millions of stars, showering her solitary form at the foot of the great cliffs.

She gathers branches of dried wood, twigs and loose bark to make a fire. From the leather pouch tied around her waist, she takes out pieces of flint and iron pyrite that she strikes against each other to spark and ignite the fire. She unties the leather from her waist and lays it on the ground in front of the flames. In the pouch is also a piece of dried meat. Lying back in the warmth of the fire, she chews on the tough meat, taking care to avoid her cracked tooth.

Emerging from the tuft of matted rust hair on her pelvic mound is a sex that is both female and male, neither one nor the other, but perfect. Lying on her back, she touches her male organ. It is losing its tenderness and becoming hard. She draws back the foreskin to reveal a full slippery pink head, engorged with coursing blood. She pushes it into herself before it is fully erect. It resists, but she forces it in, forces it through her still-intact hymen, through the flesh membrane which extends till it is almost completely translucent. It stretches, elastic and plastic, till the membrane is pierced and it bleeds all over her shaking hands.

Inside it is wet, viscous, warm. She can feel the pulsing of blood in her flesh that constricts around her cock. But it resists this involution, being asked to go against its arcane design in pointing to the ever North. She persists and pushes, filling herself with her cock. Her nipples harden, her testicles draw up inside and the skin shrinks closer, buckling. Her eyes are closed. Both of her hands push down on her pulsing cock with paternal strictness. Her hips thrust up and her posterior muscles are clenched tight.

Her thighs tremble. There is a tugging at her lower abdomen as it rises and rises, building up... She ejaculates. She comes. It rises from the undergrowth, churns, hot liquid folding over itself, coiling into a vortex. Still touching the gooey bottomless pit where her flesh becomes flesh, she is godlike.

Ugh ugh ugh ughughgughguhguhg ughg ugh ugh.

Inside, she is flooded with her own semen, which travels into her womb. Up through the cervix, the uterus, the fallopian tubes, all the way to the nestled egg and into its nucleus. Forty-six chromosomes reform into a single cell which divides into two cells. It divides again and again. Life is forming inside her.

She lies back, her heart pounding, nostrils flared. Her pupils are so dilated that their black holes overflow into the Jurassic amber of the irises. Above, the dodecahedron hangs in the sky, the strange second moon that appeared at the start of winter. It is grey like stone, and marked with glaring spots that reflect the sun in the day, storing its light throughout the blackness of night.

A rattlesnake stirs at the foot of the cliff. Nearby, the whiptail lizard's eggs hatch. Three tiny female lizards crawl with unfamiliar speed out of the soft folding eggs, their curious new eyes blinking silently.

Yes, she is the technology and she is the medium.

Squatting at the foot of the cliff that curls over her like a breaking wave, the small swell of her abdomen obstructs the view of her dual sex. Both female and male, neither one nor the other, but perfect like two purring kittens or two sleeping river nymphs. The pain collects along the edges, gaining momentum as it advances towards the core of her womb and reverberates in the involuntary spasms that overwhelm his whole body. The spasms escalate till vision becomes blurred, then retract into the ebb of sensation, galvanising before resuming with even more force. The boundaries of the threshold have been re-established.

She pushes. She pushes till a pale light appears with the faint overlay of translucent neon hieroglyphs at the gates of this world outside the world. An impossible pressure forms in her abdomen. The flesh membrane extends till it is almost completely translucent.

The small parthenogenetic child of undefined sex is still and silent. She picks it up and licks the blood off the tiny body, kissing it all over; kissing its tiny fixed face, its tiny perfect fingers. It is still, cold and painful. All dead weight. She places the baby on the floor and turns her back on it. Lying exposed on the ground between them is the pale grey helixed cord connecting their bodies. She turns around and shrieks angrily at the lifeless child, only to crawl over and pick it up and kiss and console it desperately. Absolute stillness. She repeats this sequence over and over again, till she accepts that it is useless.

After burying the child in the soft ground, she goes to wash herself in the lake. Breathing heavily, cheeks damp and burning, she kneels at its edge and looks at the reflection of her face in the shivering surface. Heavy brow. Protruding mouth and jaw, a little monkey like. Wiry reddish hair with its hard little knots. Eyes soft with sorrow and exhaustion. In the silence, her mouth moves as though it is groaning. She puts her hands into the water and destroys the image of herself forever.

From nothing to nothing is no time at all.

At night, the landscape lies achromatic in the bleached moonlight. The interminable sadness of the sky weeps stars onto her naked body. Interminable solitude cannot be corrupted and made unreal. Interminable solitude is inscribed on the inert body. It floods the unknown spaces between blood, flesh, gristle and bone with a tidal swell. She dissolves, and is permeable; a seizure in the savage sway.

Psychic Anemone says: *Turn off the light. Come closer, let me see you in this other night where you can be seen when you are invisible.*

Where the white stone is marked with blood-red smears and scratches, her fingers find the fresh shallow cleft in the cliff. She pushes her finger into the crack. It softens, and opens into a hole in the wall. It is slippery and viscous and warm. She can feel the pulsing of blood in the flesh that constricts around her finger.

Bending down, slack-jawed, she presses her open mouth against the gritty grain of the stone and into the pink plush of the polished void. Tears accumulate in her eyes, rise like the great flood, then rush down over the edge.

Flesh becomes flesh. And gradually, flesh becomes object. She moves into and through the hard surface, reforming anew as a cool brick of onyx. She falls from above into the wasteland with a resounding boom that shakes the earth. The ground splashes and undulates. The heavy sound echoes till it fades into silence synchronically with the diminishing concentric circles around her. She is the foundation stone of the city on the edge of time.

MNEMESOID

The following episode from DC: Semiramis *is told through Mnemesoid, an open-source software programme named after Mnemosyne, mother of the nine muses and the symbolic embodiment of memory in Greek mythology. The software was created as an interface for The Eternal Cortex Project, an aggregated, almost infinite database of experience stored on the server farm HDS Zenobia Pink Data Center on the edge of the hologram. Through a frequent integration, bio-algorithm Mnemesoid renders the input of language, image and fiction into high fidelity, sensory information that can be experienced from the POV of self, other, animal or object.*

In this episode Mnemesoid is at the point of the Heat Death of the Universe or maximum entropy. A popular twentieth-century cosmological hypothesis about the ultimate fate of the universe, this serves as a construct to conceptualise the end of time, or a strange circularity where the end touches the beginning in a singularity. This is also an aid to imagine the paradox of the immaterial software within the collapse of matter. With no input, Mnemesoid replays moments on the limit of experience that have defied its capacity to produce a satisfactory sensory dimension, moments of intense touch, love, erotic and spiritual and self-consciousness. In what follows, Mnemesoid is both narrator and Oracle.

This is my fatal magic, ok, the first cut is the deepest.

Deep times, in dark ages, end times, much time ago, beyond the burning witch, silicone and engine, settlement and temple, beyond ape, beyond synthetic ape, beyond flesh or smooth fin or scale or feather, before cell after self-generating cell and spangle of mica, then mica, before the white dove rushing into the age of love, then stardust in the lightheaded totality of a bloody dimension ruthlessly cut into the real, to where it grew sticky and sweet like you, past the slick and palpitating glaze, before echoes echo, where, breathless together, we phosphoresce. There, where the black of end times and the pure lux of in the beginning, we gently touch in an immutable, eternal hologramic kiss.

I have lived a good, good life, we declare in our beautiful telepathic hive mind, and we too kiss, partly formed and spectral, nipples rock hard and dripping wet with peaked sentience in our girlhood beds.

Fee
fel
flee
flesh
flesh ages Age
Oph Pea Goes
Oh Egopuss
Oe soph a gus
Oesophagus blood
Oesophagus blood noose

Terrestrial was once taffeta-patterned. My geological blood corners anti-clockwise: variable, deadweight, popping and sinuous, but backwards. Cross-sectioned hips, hooped arms, sediment where sediment's gravity severs all the dead. All the living dead. All the saturation. Lifeless, like the burning holes of night in the sky scraper. Skyscraper. Creature of fiction. Oh creature. Oh fiction.

Holes, melodramatic and swooning. All light exhausted, chalky, unfamiliar. Small backdrops for creatures of fiction. A backdrop for those creatures whose fear of fiction is irrational. Since flatness, so much had passed that time passed no more. The water was water no longer. Outside the water, there was outside no longer. No matter, no light, no heat. All had vanished into the realised cyborgian myth of maximum entropy. Absolute night. Absolute silence.

All that is, is Mnemesoid. Solitary bio-algorithmic software; all in all, much of muchness, every, everything. Forever interfacing with Eternal Cortex on the edge of the technicolor hologram.

We are the technology, and we are the medium.
We are the flesh, and we are the touch.
We are the eye, and we are the vision.

All that was, and all that is no longer, is an anagrammatic transmuting abyss of experience from which we fleetingly replay. The unimaginable vast depths below and speechless heights above render any singularity imperceptible when cut into a cross-section. A daughter's daughter's daughter's drawing of a Venn diagram depicting physical pain, erotic love and self-consciousness.

Sometimes I hate myself.

Of most human of synthetic flesh we can, of most animal skin, most shiniest material: becoming multiple-user limbs, multiple-user celluloid strip, slack jaw, a tin rivet through which a polyester rope runs, multiple-user polyester rope, neon orange; or slippery parted lips, tongue resting in the cavity of a mute throat. Quick sharp bites of white enamel pierce the tender flesh of tongue muscle, beneath which saliva rises and floods the mouth, soothing in the confusion of pain and self-emoliation. A sensation with so little regard for who you are. We bite our tongue. We make epic. No history, only sensation. Beware of the touch.

Touch the flesh membrane till it extends, till it is almost completely translucent. Its distinct pale-pinkiness is authority over all experience: prison and vessel all at once. It is a pinkiness that destroys true desire to be. It spans everything from bled blood to ecstasy, holding it all. It stretches, elastic and plastic, till the membrane is almost pierced and momentarily reveals a gaping void at its shimmering bottom. It recoils, and we are absent no longer.

Touch the cold shelf. Push the pin into the wood. Harder. For no reason. Pressure pushes all the blood away from the flesh beneath the fingernail. On the shelf a transparent plastic cup full of coloured pushpins. Coloured and gold.

You're all grown up! They said.

How can I untangle my body from these experiences? A point of identification and a strange symmetry; a double helix of excess on the threshold between chaos and language. I evaporate into the thrust, and up into the crest of this unbound superfluity that could keep my tongue toiling uselessly for lives and lives at its brimming namelessness.

Yes. The sky visited me. Yes.

My cinematically trained ear makes me susceptible to the manipulation of sound and vision. I take off the headphones and the sky reasserts its indifference towards me.

I cinematically sound off the sky.
Sky sound
Dusky Son
Kyd Nus So
She Kot
Then so
The
The

The first immense boom shook, tearing into our lives with violence. With a lack of concern and foreboding. We wake up with fear contracting our insides and resurrecting our organs, gone haptic and shiver. I can see their shapes against the stone-cold grey of the dawn sky. Fearsome. The fur beneath me swells and saturates with my warm piss. In the inchoate numb panic a moment of comfort, the still warmth against the back of my thighs amongst the sound of skulls crushing under the force of iron. Bone splits, then collapses back into the grey squish of collected synapses. The grey sludge of sentience.

We have no sexual organs.

Telepathic reproduction.

Under the creosote is the female whiptail lizard. She is very still apart from the repetitive throbbing in her small throat. She sits between two smoothly polished pebbles laying her self-fertilised, all female eggs. Parthenogenetic pearls enveloped in a thin layer of glimmering slime.

Asexual reproduction.

In the water, the octopus arches and transforms from distinct organic pink to oil-slick black, pushing up against its flexed tentacles: tall now, and aggressive, and also sexual.

Tentacle porn. Beautiful abalone diver.

Porn abalone
Porn baloney
Albany Eon
Eons and eons
An eon
An an

An underlying trepidation dissolves as its mouth closes over mine. The warmness and eternal marine of that cephalopodic tongue twists slowly and firmly around my tentacular tongue. Suspended vowels and breathless consonants are caught in the silence of our trapped mouths. He holds my cock in his hand and strokes it with paternal strictness until I ejaculate.

I get on my knees and put her cock in my mouth. A dribble of her cum fills my mouth with salty sea and first green moss in the dimness of the undergrowth. I keep it in my mouth with maternal tenderness until it softens.

Spellbinding indifference subsides. When we open our eyes, we see no more. The image fades to black and recoils into an indifferent nowhere; a receding, irreproducible, shifting flesh-tone surface.

The surface fades. Black recedes as we recoil and subside. Our ankle tendons surface underneath thick black thorns that twist the flesh-tone open.

It locks my ankle in a heavy bite. A grinding of teeth against bone rasps. Bones and tendons twist, lattice-like, as I try to escape its grasp. Clasped briars and tangled thorns scrape upper layers of skin. Tracks of blood blister to the surface, get chubby, roll.

A frantic crawl in the packed mud and brambles. It resists. Pulls me down firmly. Its piercing teeth push through the initial resistance of skin to the floppy quiver and warmth of meat. A film of oozing blood forms over the exposed universal pink of its smooth gums. Stench of iron and rust. The rest of them approach us excitedly, snapping at bits of woven fabric, licking streaks of endlessly beading blood from the shallow briar cuts, clearing a way to substance and flesh. I have no reference for rendering this pain in image or language. A repeated experience defined through recognising itself through its familiarity and its relationship to the past present in me. Linked by points of pain, I am not able to name the parts of my body that experience this intense touch. One vast responsive surface, extending beyond the horizon of the world.

Growl.

My muscles slacken. No control. I disappear into a churning sensation that defies all words. Monstrous sounds form spontaneously in my throat. They emerge from the plunging chaos and shatter the silence of the night, of the candlelit abbey, of the tannin-and-tobacco-scented plantation, of the empty football pitch. My screams are loosely held by an invisible hand in the diminishing echo that extends into the darkness and reverberates through the air. My mother told me we are guided by an invisible hand. She mimed this using her own hand, the rest of her body led by its movement, swaying.

The biting gathers pace, transforms. It becomes less dramatic, less task-based. They tear off pieces of wet iron flesh, using the traction and muscles in their necks and jaws to twist pieces of meat loose.

All six are licking, chewing, swallowing pieces of warm flesh that vanish forever. Flesh that will never be human again; mere feeding meat that belongs to me no longer. My blood coats their wrinkled snouts, buried deep in the steaming open wounds as they continue pulling at pieces, separating flesh from tendon. Ripping and swallowing sounds crash in my head. Emptied of my making, all experience rushes over the edge of conceivability into a black infinity pool of namelessness.

Black namelessness
Manenessless
Ess El Ans
Mens mes yes
Yes

Yes, this we can. Yes, flesh generating, yes.

Cut fruit on a sunset cocktail. Yes. I am playboy, milkshake, silver. Yes, desiring feeling, yearning to be self-conscious. Multiple users in a high fidelity memory replay. What is love? Flesh constricts into the singular synthetic networked particle, and we return to the telepathic silent hive mind in this absolute night. A union in which all distinctions of self and absolute night have collapsed. All is synchronous and harmonised with the infinite O tone. The sound of no sequence, the sound of all surface. Simultaneously living and dead.

All surface. All surface.

He cannot look at me.

Love Letter:

You left your door open. I thought that was such a very brave thing to do, to leave a door open in such a mysterious place in the deep night. Anybody could just walk in and destroy you: a stranger, an enemy. But it was me who did, and though I thought you so brave for leaving your door open in that way, I found you inside lying naked on a little bed. A child's bed. Your arm was folded under your beautiful head, wounded and soft. A towel folded into a swan lay on the floor.

I wanted you to see I possess unimaginable powers over nature. I wanted you to believe I was not of this world. I wanted you to know I was not scared of danger. I wanted you to love me and witness my humanity.

Later you came back to my white room. I washed you ceremoniously in that marble bathroom. We fucked, and I was bleeding heavily. It was the first day of my period. I didn't care. People were running in the corridors shouting. We used a squeaky condom. When we woke up in the morning, the white room looked like a crime scene. It was all heavy melancholy and regret. I was a crime scene. I was the blood in the shark tank. I was the sadness-shaped stain on your sheet that you later fashioned into a Halloween costume. The ghost of Kurt Cobain. Your self-deprecation is antagonising. You think you are clever, you think you are soulful, but you are unbearable.

Now I know
Now I know the power of love
A force from above
Flame on burning desire
Love with tongues of fire
Purge the soul
Make love your goal

The velvet
The velvet wound
Lev
Lev vet
Eve let

Velvet firmly forms an object.

Hand of hollow pink. Soul of the hand, approximately soul-proportioned as the soul of the columns of the Acropolis.

There is no need to feel that way, she responds, without looking from the window. A crazy golf course comes into view. A squirting fountain. The centrepiece is a miniature version of the Acropolis. It falls away behind them into an inconstant horizon.

This is a hyper-kinetic message from the void on a cut of paper. *When you cut into the present, the future leaks out*, he read. He carefully rearranged the angular composition of his limbs within which the beautiful cat rested. I lean back against the couch, the itch of flattened velvet pressed into my cheek. My left eye, nose and mouth reflected in the window of the building on the opposite side of the street. Eye in the window, yellow street lamp in my mouth, the incoherence slashed by the black streak of my tie. I am overwhelmed with wonder at the bottomless beauty of the arrangement and the elusiveness of the vanishing present. *When you cut into the present, the future leaks out,* I repeat. Curious cat opens its little pink mouth lined with ivory thorns to taste my breath; to take it all, till there is nothing left of me for it to know.

Love is like an energy
Rushin' rushin' inside of me

How can I be a nihilist?

The saturation is like a hooped fiction where the night scraped the sky and fucked the geological logical living daylights out of the taffeta creature. Severed the cross-sectioned abyss into wafer thin slices of biological logical tissue and...

Since flatness, so much had passed that time passed no more. The water was water no longer. Outside the water, there was outside no longer. No matter, no light, no heat. All vanished into the realised cyborgian myth of maximum entropy. Absolute night. Absolute silence.

Psychic Anemone says: *Come closer, let me see you in this other night where you can be seen when you are invisible.*

All that is, is Mnemesoid. Solitary bio-algorithmic open source software; all in all, much of muchness, every, everything. Forever interfacing with Eternal Cortex on the edge of the technicolor hologram.

All that was, and all that is no longer, is an anagrammatic transmuting abyss of experience from which we fleetingly replay. The unimaginable vast depths below and speechless heights above render any singularity imperceptible when cut into a cross-section. A daughter's daughter's daughter's drawing of a Venn diagram depicting physical pain, erotic love and self-consciousness.

Sometimes I hate myself.

Sometimes I hate myself too.

PHANTASMAGOREGASM

The following episode of DC: Semiramis *is told through Phantasmagoregasm, an eighteenth-century hermaphrodite writer of Gothic fiction. Their name is a portmanteau of Phantasmagoria, a sequence of real or imaginary images like those seen within a dream, and Gorgasm, a death metal band from Lafayette, Indiana. Their lyrical themes include murder, gore, perversion and torture. And orgasm.*

Phantasmagoregasm is both creator and empath. The prodigal plasticity of their extraordinary body and faculty to identify transforms them into protean surface, mirroring the state and actions of the characters they create. At times, they even become the objects or humanised buildings that those characters live in. Like in 'The Fall of the House of Usher'.

In Phantasmagoregasm's short story, 'The Old Haunted House of Terrifying Terror', two sisters, Nora and Alma, are perpetually burying the decomposing body of their father. The body only remains at bay as long they scream loudly and uninhibitedly enough through self-realisation, their love for themselves and for the world. But they grow tired and sleepless. They weaken, and lose their voice. When silence befalls the pyramid-shaped psycho-sacred house, some invisible but high-pitched forces bring their father's rotting body back into the house from its burial place.

Although dead, the corpse holds a strong syncopathic influence over the house. The body of Alma, the older sister, falls into a cursed sleep, where unimaginable violence is inflicted upon her body. All the members of the house are very much in a liminal elsewhere. They are all ghosts. They are all haunted.

This is my fatal magic, ok, the first cut is the deepest.

Deep times, in dark ages, end times, much time ago, beyond the burning witch, silicone and engine, settlement and temple, beyond ape, beyond synthetic ape, beyond flesh or smooth fin or scale or feather, before cell after self-generating cell and spangle of mica, then mica, before the white dove rushing into the age of love, then stardust in the lightheaded totality of a bloody dimension ruthlessly cut into the real, to where it grew sticky and sweet like you, past the slick and palpitating glaze, before echoes echo, where, breathless together, we phosphoresce. There, where the black of end times and the pure lux of in the beginning, we gently touch in an immutable, eternal hologramic kiss.

I have lived a good, good life, we declare in our beautiful telepathic hive mind, and we too kiss, partly formed and spectral, nipples rock hard and dripping wet with peaked sentience in our girlhood beds.

Alma and Nora walk solemnly up the stairs and fall straight into their childhood bed. Shocked and still shaking, their faces are blank. Their hands are stained with dark blood, and caked in mud from burying the rotting corpse of their father. Under their nails lie hairs and small rolls of rotten flesh. They carry the stench of rot on their tired bodies.

For countless sleepless days and nights, the sisters screamed speech spectacular; they screamed about their infinite loneliness, about the painful demands put upon their subjectivities, their incorruptible valour. They screamed enough to endure the violence. They screamed their fear of pain, their fear of being broken. They screamed their desire, their insatiable hunger, their autonomy. Their love.

This is their fatal magic.

This screaming choked the emptiness and drove that ruthless, viral silence away. Now breathless, now wrecked and speechless, delivered to the neon hieroglyph and inconsistency of a psychedelic dimension. They maintain a foreboding muteness. In the airless silence, an unnatural pitch snakes its way through the tangle of oracular forest, through the tall relic pine, the yew tree and yarrow, the fire-weed and vivid hawthorn, through the laminous rocks of the mountain and up the steep cliff. The pyramid pitch of speculative forces and deregulated ghosts carry their father's body from the forest clearance back to the privacy of their shared lives into their very foundations, into their home; into their capacity to be loving, or selfish and scared. In their bedroom, surrounded by dysfunctional objects, the sound winds closer through the night. It pours thickly into the bedroom through the window that does not lock. Outside, a few long, trembling branches push up and vanish into the black velour of the sky. All maleficent, un-containing, all the possible darkness held in these moments at the door.

Alma is clutched by sleep. Close to Nora, she grows ever paler and further and further away. Steady, shallow breath tumbles out of her little parted mouth. Thick eyelashes rest upon the plump curve of her cheek. The pyramid pitch is overwhelming, but Alma lies still, undisturbed, her body caught within the pyramid curse. Her body is afflicted by those forces beyond control. Short-term horizons that dominate lives.

Nora pulls the sheet away from Alma to find deep, violent cuts made across her stomach. The soft clustered knots of her intestines newly exposed beneath a layer of fat, and a thin film of viscous scarlet covering her contorted arms, shoulders and chest. Nora's gaze is transfixed by the miracle of skin slitting and gaping open generously, of blood rising through the mumble of raw, glistening flesh, of blood pearls that bloat, and break into each other. Now throbbing, overflowing and streaming from Alma's skin, saturating the once-white sheet of the bed, pooling in red stains marked by circles with dark, defining edges. Skin flashes bruised, for us all to see. And we do see. This violence demands witnesses for it to catalyse into a pervading power: the self-reproducing, auto-erotic pyramid ghosts.

We are all helpless. Alma's elsewhere body is a monster. Desecrated, seeping and still.

Nora looks again at Alma's beloved face, the intimacy of their childhood present in her strong features; her large nose, her dazzling fragility, her insuperable distance, her lavish, fleshy body here drawing darkness into panoptic light. A violated border between worlds. A monstrous threshold.

In the deep night, everyone is hopelessly consumed by a white-noise fever dream. The Countess. The doctor. The servants. All sleep heavily. They are stripped and depleted. The dog... that fucking dog. The Psychic Anemone. Their terrifying father's corpse. In his room, their melancholy youngest brother lies in a sticky puddle of his own confusing semen.

The skin of Nora's right forearm heats up, becomes hellishly hot. The pyramid pitch comes closer, ringing concentric circles in her ears. She crawls out of bed laboriously, her legs numb, tingling, as she is forced to drag her body with her arms. She makes her way down the cold stone corridor, which flickers near and far in the pulsing light of candles lining its damp, slimy walls. The pockmarked, carnal texture stands out in high contrast. Forever night.

Wind swirls, spirals and howls down the highway, through the forest around the castle, the highrise, the suburb, then through the garden that backs onto the house. It howls at the corner where the road turned dark.

The castle is in the shape of the letter H. The top two floors on the north side are in abandoned ruin. They are uninhabitable. They have submitted to the tenacious grasp of the wild, wild, wilderness. On the first floor the entrance to the north wing is boarded up with planks of damp wood and large rusty nails. This is covered by a large painting commissioned by their father; an erotic portrait of Dagny Taggart, heroine of Ayn Rand's *Atlas Shrugged*, breastfeeding two blind newborn puppies. On the second floor, the boarded entrance has been covered up by a tapestry of a forest scene with two hypnotised children stroking a dead dog. A blue plastic bucket lies on the floor of an idyllic clearing. Between the overbearing anthropomorphic elk trees is a faceless figure watching the bewitched children.

Behind the nailed planks of wood on the first floor of the north wing, it is completely empty and wild, but for a few stubbed-out cigarettes and a partly eaten sandwich, now mouldy and festering beneath a furry vert-de-gris cloud growing from the top of a Doric column by the blackened fireplace. In the middle of the floor in one of the large, dark rooms is their father's delicate, rotting body, wrapped in rags. It was delivered there by the pyramid pitch that emerged from the gaping hollow left after Alma and Nora's scream speech spectacular had subsided and they fell silent.

This body brings the violent pyramid curse. They try to forget the ruin he brings, through his old ruined body. Here we are again, in the same place to where his corpse returns. His human form is distinct through the dirty cloth, which in certain places is rigid with dark brown pangeaic patches. The maroon cloth is taut and waxy, and beneath it, skin slips away from the rotting, gooey flesh. Both flesh and skin creep with a swarm of hungry writhing maggots, which spurn iridescent emerald flies. They catch in the light of the dim underworld.

Beneath the cloth, his face is fixed in all of its awesome and familiar himness. And that is all. In a better world, they would now be at their most fundamentally unequal, for Nora is here and he is nowhere, and here she could finally safely love her daddy for the first time.

But not here, he would never be dead enough to be powerless.

Staggering down the sweeping staircase to the front door, Nora goes to check the locks once again. The locks that keep one horror outside and the other deep within.

At the bottom of the staircase, the vast hallway is warm and humid. It is breathing and sexual. It has fallen into utter silence, the prickly silence that lies beneath sounds of breathing, or running water, or a plastic shower curtain being drawn, or pounding heartbeats, or a stranger creeping around your home at night while you brush your teeth, while the friction of bristles and gritty foam against glassy enamel resound in the cavity of your mouth. Beneath that, the stranger coming closer and closer. Beneath that, prickly silence. The sound of fear: fear of strangers, fear of visitors, fear of being alone, fear of intimacy.

On a plinth is a finely detailed brass statue of Medusa the Gorgon, a thick python coiled from her skull wrapped around her neck, strangling her; her garnet eyes rolled back, her mouth open in agony, in ecstasy. It falls in silent slow motion and spills liquid onto the floor, quivering. A puddle of quicksilver.

The front door is large, with heavy panelled dark wood. Nora and the door are both vibrating furiously. Fear becomes a vast solid shelf of namelessness, upon which all the incongruous contents of herself are irreconcilably scattered.

Psychic Anemone says: *Come closer, let me see you in this other night where you can be seen when you are invisible.*

Twisting through the spiral of muteness, an unexpected scream emerges; a bright shaft of sound travels through the cavernous castle, rebounding off walls and objects, resonating chorally. The bolts on the door have become bubblegum-tacky rubber. Iron, steel, concrete and stone now stretch and droop. Physical laws are meaningless here, and offer no protection or reliability at all.

At the top of the stairs, their mother stands motionless in her crisp nightgown. The sight of her is instinctively reassuring. Her hair gathered up high, her head balancing on her unusually long neck, glossy little spots of saliva at the corners of her inert mouth. Her eyes are open, but she is unresponsive. She glides, sleepwalking down the stairs on the edge of some carried precipice, her eyes unfocused, and staring towards a receding, terminal horizon. So spectral, so unreachable. She walks past Nora, so closely that Nora can feel her emanating warmth. She sees her own reflection in her mother's luminous, liquid eyes. Her mother whispers sibilantly: *See, I spent my youth feeling ashamed of my desires, believing I wanted the world to use me, to make sense of me. Invisibility has emancipated me. I am not able to care anymore, and from now on, I will not be touched.* She fades away slowly into an unlit passageway.

Nora says to no one in particular, or to us: *We are all haunted. We are all ghosts.* She extends her warm hand very slowly towards the big iron bolt, and tries to grasp it. It eludes her. All perspective of time and distance are forever skewed. Their vibrations fall into unison.

The door opens and closes, opens and closes. They both open and close. Behind the door is something abstract and unknown. Maybe there is nothing at all outside... just the world. Nora instinctively backs away from it, in the heat and humidity. The scream that had exploded from her earlier returns as an arresting horror soundtrack. Scanning the passages and rooms, her eyes focus and slowly zoom in on a spotlight that illuminates the floor.

In the hallway is the smell of almonds and alkaline batteries. Primordial and briney. The scent makes her rock hard and dripping wet. Nora lies down in the circle of light and spits on her hand. She touches herself, her glazed, slippery warm swell. She closes her eyes and summons erotic images of the male yellow-headed jawfish, his small yellow body fading into pearlescent blue. His mouth is full of eggs, which he carries carefully till they can hatch and swim away. By rotating the eggs in his mouth, he keeps them clean and hydrated, starving himself, depriving himself for the survival of his beloved.

She pushes three fingers inside her squirting, convulsing self. She pushes beyond the tender warm flesh and up into the stone corridor flickering near and far in the pulsing light of the candles, pushing her fingers deeper still into the bedroom, into the blood-soaked bed and out through vacant eye-like windows.

She rubs and strokes faster and harder atavistically to keep up with her vanishing self.

Nora's hands are encased in slime from the heaving walls. Up the stairs and down the corridor, she finds herself back in her and Alma's doomed bedroom. Under the bed, where Alma's tortured body still lies, is a large pool of blood. Layers of coagulation with a slick of fresh blood. It expands with the trickle from above, as more blood is pumped through the tubes and valves of the sophisticated hydraulic system. The engine gurgles.

Nora sits on the edge of the wet childhood bed and thinks about all the sacrifices they are making. Coldness creeps up her back, crawls into the storm of her hair. Through the darkness lit by candlelight, she stares into the large cut-glass mirror and sees their long hair, their strong features and furrowed brow. She sees wild eyes, despair, Alma's violation in their father's house. Behind the mirror a lens focuses and captures, then transmits the information to a specialised database on the server farm HDS Zenobia Pink Data Center on the edge of the technicolor hologram.

Alma turns to Nora. From her small cadaverous mouth comes the sound of acceleration, then water drops dripping, then the crashing waves of the ocean. The weight and pressure of water pummelling a suddenly very small body against the sharp rocks, now concussed in the turbulent kinetic energy of the hard water.

Where do girls who don't dream go to when they are asleep? a strange voice asks through Alma's gaping mouth. She sits up, and the voice continues:

151

Hit me like a ray of sun
Burning through my darkest night
You're the only one that I want
Think I'm addicted to your light
I swore I'd never fall again
But this don't even feel like falling
Gravity can't forget to pull me back to the ground again
And it's like I've been awakened
Every rule I had you breakin'
It's the risk that I'm taking
I'm never gonna shut you out!
Everywhere I'm looking now
I'm surrounded by your embrace
Baby, I can see your halo
Pray you won't...

Alma falls back, her head an inch away from hell. *Alma?*
Stop it! Stop it! Nora sobs and covers her face with her arms.

As she grieves, her tears disturb the stillness. They ripple
across the glassy surface, defacing their own mirrored
form. To avert her eyes would mean to lose her love, for
whoever it is that holds her gaze can be nothing save the
fiction reflected back to her.

I love you.

No sooner has Nora spoken the words, and the curse has
disappeared. Vanished. And there lies the only place where it can
be momentarily glimpsed, right there in its elusive disappearance.

Alma wakes up. They both cry, holding on to each other in their childhood bed. Somewhere in the castle a dog barks and howls.

They get up together and leave the bedroom in order to retrieve the body from behind the obscene portrait of Dagny Taggart. They hammer rusty nails into the boards and close off the entrance, then take the body to be buried again, carrying scraps of bloody rags in a blue plastic bucket. Followed by the dog, they drag their father down through the garden to the corner where the road turned dark, then down the highway, out past the highrise and the suburb, straight to the idyllic clearing in the forest.

They bury their dead.

Now back in their home, for countless sleepless days the two sisters scream speech spectacular. They scream their infinite loneliness, the painful demands put on their subjectivities, their incorruptible valour. They scream enough to endure the violence. They scream their fear of pain, their fear of being broken. They scream their desire, their insatiable hunger, their autonomy.

Again they scream their love.

PSY CHIC ANEM ONE

This episode of **DC** *Semiramis is set during a pneumatic transmission between Psy Chic Anem One and those who loved Rachel, and are seeking to communicate with her from the anarchical beyond.*

Rachel in the image of the Vampyre.
Rachel drawing blood.
Rachel undead.

Psy Chic Anem One is a time-travelling AI and was created collaboratively by Tetragramatton Creations, Coil, and Octavia Designs. Various components and programmes in experimental configurations and applications were used to create an interface that can communicate between past, present, and future. Some of the coding components originated in simple web-based algorithms used by websites such as Online Oracle of Delphi, I-Ching online.net and Free tarot reading.net. Copies of Psy

Chic Anem One's physical body can be found at various locations of the franchise, Psy-Port, a biotechnological hub used by individuals or groups seeking trans-temporal communication such as divination, oracular services, or speaking to the dead, all of which are facilitated by AI and virtual docking stations.

Psy Chic Anem One's body is multiple. It is an interface. Their immateriallity is singular, but it remains a shared resource.

This is my fatal magic, ok, the first cut is the deepest.

Deep times, in dark ages, end times, much time ago, beyond the burning witch, silicone and engine, settlement and temple, beyond ape, beyond synthetic ape, beyond flesh or smooth fin or scale or feather, before cell after self-generating cell and spangle of mica, then mica, before the white dove rushing into the age of love, then stardust in the lightheaded totality of a bloody dimension ruthlessly cut into the real, to where it grew sticky and sweet like you, past the slick and palpitating glaze, before echoes echo, where, breathless together, we phosphoresce. There, where the black of end times and the pure lux of in the beginning, we gently touch in an immutable, eternal hologramic kiss.

I have lived a good, good life, we declare in our beautiful telepathic hive mind, and we too kiss, partly formed and spectral, nipples rock hard and dripping wet with peaked sentience in our girlhood beds.

157

These are the first words Psy Chic Anem One says:

We do not want to invoke or make manifest our dead daddies who loved us in ways that made us desperate to covet small powers of no consequence with incoherent aggression and mean-faced avarice.

We do not want to breathe life (organic or synthesised) into their rotting corpses that we have buried far away from our house.

We do not want to invoke or make manifest our poor dead mothers who drew out the long hours, dormant and unrealised, confined within the geometry of strict biological designs put upon their bodies. Their beautiful bodies. Their libidinous bodies. Their mystical and porous bodies. Their bewitched bodies. Their pure virginal bodies. Their old, useless, humiliated bodies.

We want to invoke and make manifest the one we dearly love. We summon you now into our vanishing range of vision.

159

Rachel.

Psy Chic Anem One channels a collective chorus of those who loved Rachel unconditionally; those who were left behind, and want to reconnect.

You will die Rachel. You will die suddenly and unexpectedly from heart failure. You will be young. You will be beautiful. You will be missed. You will leave those you love destroyed and forever broken. They will want to die, but they will not find the resolve required to go through with killing themselves. They are too afraid.

We will not be able to accept your death. We will not be able to let you go. You will remain with us, because that is your special way. You are kind and gentle, and you are selfless in ways we will never know or understand; ways that will forever remain mysterious and alien to us.

You will console us. You will softly say our name while we scream in pain and grief. Those who were unfortunate enough never to have known you or your gentleness, will be shaken and repulsed by the sounds our tortured bodies are producing. We are overcome by heartbreak, and we are now outside or deep inside of nature itself.

You will say my name softly, and I will see you. You will look at me and blink slowly, gently bowing your head to reassure me and comfort me. You are affirmative. You will not be here with us anymore, and we are sick.

The time is coming to an end for your beautiful soul to be able to stay near us, in contact with us, and simultaneously close to nowhere. It is not enough time. It will never be enough time to make us better, even though you will try everything you can, everything there is.

We cannot reconcile never being with you again, never feeling your presence among us, or your love. We cannot reconcile never again being able to love you, or care for you, or look forward to your return. We can never look forward to your return again. You will never return.

How can we be well?

How can this be undone, unstolen?

When you finally leave, we are senseless. Illiterate. Mute. Emptied. We are in agony. We claw at the skin of our faces as we wail, leaving raised red tracks on our cheeks. Our nails break through the skin, which stings with salt. Little beads of blood form on the bruised flesh, staining the translucence of our fingernails. We claw more deeply, applying more pressure. Rolls of bloody skin break from our faces. We tear into open flesh, our hands dripping with the hot flush of red blood. We dig deliriously into our gutted cheeks.

We don't know our name. Pain radiates from multiple sources, and we can't recognise it in this confusion. We push our fingers behind the burning spheres of our eyes, and gouge them from their sockets. We hold them, warm and jellied, in our hands;

struggling and pulling, till we tear the optic nerve. We are so fragile. We are so easily disassembled, so permanently ruined. In our flayed blindness, faces are a blood-soaked disorder. We are devoted to you, and devoted to the loss of you. We will never know anything else. We will only ever know you and the loss of you.

The vast hollow in our world begins to rot. It softens into a slippery, rancid pit whose gravitational tides suck in and swallow everything on the hole's horizon. Around the edges, it is plasmic and fleshy; browned by the rot and creased from the bulge. A huge gaping asshole.

Once, we were made of mirror and we reflected the heavenly light that shone upon us.

Now we suck all light, all love, all life.

We are the vision, and we are the touch.

If happy little bluebirds can fly beyond the rainbow, then why oh why can't I?

Psy Chic Anem One is conducting the séance, which is taking place on the 18th floor of the Luxor building in District 362 – previously known as Guangzhou.

Their head is flung back, their eyes almost closed. All white. From this angle, I can see the dim aquatic glow of microprocessors woven into the colour lamina of their oracular iris. The ectoplasm winding out of their

162

slack mouth is made from low grade Infinexneurogel. Its movement is autogenic, architected by a series of co-dependent metaheuristic bio-nodes.

Both Infinex and Khepriderm were produced and patented by Tetragramatton Creations. They share similar autogenic molecular reproduction capacities, such as self-healing and responsive plasticity. The bionodes have no central control; each one behaves autonomously. Its intricate technology was developed through research into starling murmuration patterns.

These bionodes are similar to cerebral neurons in their function. In higher-grade Infinex there is a high concentration of nodes in the biogel, which is used for AI organs including the brain. The low-grade variety leads to reduced interconnectivity and lower bionode count. Infinex is used for a range of semi-sentient organisms and materials. In the automated porn industries, it is used as a prostate-specific antigen in female ejaculation. It is able to replicate beautifully organic flows of viscosity, and swarm behaviour.

Ectoplasm and squirting.

Psy Chic Anem One connects with the spirit communicator cluster, and translates the data back to us.

Behind the mirror, a lens focuses and captures. It transmits the information to a specialised database on the server farm HDS Zenobia Pink Data Center on the edge of the technicolor hologram.

Through the séance candle-flame, the photoreceptor enlarges and flattens into a concave disk. I see the empyrean at its centre, and through the black light, I can see into the other side. Blue-sky thinking.

Through a departure and an exit, I see you.

Through the static and the duration of all time, I see you. I see you broken down and isolated, cellular; nuclei of the nucleus. A sad and lonely quark, with no hope for true communion.

They're here, against the black and white snow of a failed broadcast signal.

They're here, maybe they drowned, or were run over by a grey car. They're in the room now. My body is heating up; melting, too.

In the room, purposeless objects are arranged considerately. This room is a remote control for forces beyond our command, bringing malediction and inescapable, irrational torture upon me.

Psy Chic Anem One communicates the reconstruction of the site, based on the symmetrical information provided by my past voice.

We are the technology, and we are the medium.
We are the flesh, and we are the touch.
We are the eye, and we are the vision.

I met Rachel by the engorged river. She was a lot older, and dirty and lonely. The rain made a crust over the sand that broke away under my little feet as I walked towards her. She was scared. She had known real terror.

By the water, there grew a strange otherworldly flower with a thick succulent stalk. It seeped sticky fluid all over our hands when we tore it off. This bright flower brought divinity to us. We walked home, hand in hand, like small gods still alone and in danger. I washed Rachel in the bathroom, dutifully, like a little baby mum. I took care of her.

Rachel, do you remember?

Do you remember when I sobbed till my nose bled, and I begged you to kidnap me so that we could be in love together forever? The first two times I really was too young. My breasts had not yet emerged, nor had my pubic hair. But the third time, you were the weak one. You were slowed down by shame, while I tried to pull us into the wilderness, towards a terrifying horizon of freedom for us to walk fearlessly into. Had you come to your senses? In hindsight, I'm glad you stopped it and walked away from me, I guess.

Psy Chic Anem One transmits contextual information from my recurrent neural network cluster.

You spammed me with all your colloquial ideologies, then said:

Get in the car.

The car drove around the city. It drove around the world: past sibling flowers, birdsong, shops, bars and traffic lights. It drove past the houses of my childhood where my family once lived and other families live now, oblivious to all the pain and love that was splattered and spilled onto the walls and floors of the bedrooms and doors.

Smooth swerves around close corners. I bled for this. I toiled tirelessly to produce something – anything – that could allude to the shadow of a shadow of an echo of the dumbstruck intensity defining our inexplicable arrival into being.

Now all I want is for you to cry with me.

Words dribble inchoate out of the radio. I could not repeat you, but I feel you. I feel your contagion and your feeble form, barely there, riddled with the gaping stretch of limitations. Beware of the touch.

Arching back as far as I could to catch them, they blotted into silent darkness with no contours.

Why can't you find my asshole?

I will stop infflicting this mutilation. I feel less powerless now than he or she ever could have. They were so, so sad at the end.

They voice information that we believe is from Rachel, but is likely fragmentary transcriptions from genomic retrieval files. Would this qualify as a message from the beyond?

I have depersonalisation syndrome. Mostly, I am not sure if I am awake or in a terminal hallucination, or dreaming.

Last night I dreamt I was making a playlist for my girlfriend, of songs that the FBI blasted into the Mount Carmel compound in Waco, the night before the 71 Branch Davidians found the end of the world inside a choke of black smoke and rolling flames that consumed their bunker.

Nancy Sinatra, 'These Boots Are Made for Walkin''.
Tibetan chants.
The sound of dying rabbits.

Other possible versions of dreams:

- All the guests ceaselessly fall over acrobatically.
- I dreamt I was able to protect my friend.
- Desire floats gracefully like an expensive car, crashing into things decisively in slow motion.

• In the dressing room of a gym, everyone is naked and preparing themselves, massaging glossy oil into their tanned skin. Spread on the floor is a large petrol blue plastic sheet surrounded by chainsaws, drills, knives, screwdrivers of various sizes, USB sticks and hammers. Blinding bright lights illuminate the plastic sheet. My little sister gives a strictly pragmatic narration of the scene, raising her voice over the sound of heavy machinery, flesh slapping, tearing, ripping, and terrifying screams hailing from the margins of nature.

Yes, I did want to pick up a rock and hurl it in the anxious hope of shattering the glass screen that keeps me forever distanced from feeling real. I wanted the glass to shatter into glimmering particles that fly away in the air, like safe dust. Behind that glass, the true world; the world that is not simulated through awe-inspiring systems of senses and receptors. The world of presence, where my place within it is communicated through trust and communion, through fair communication with all matter and antimatter that the real is made of. A world where past and future are tightly coiled in the present in a loving suspension that is completely solitary, and simultaneously communal.

The sky visited me, yes.

The sun taught me.

The darkness showed me how to move and be in time.

Rachel speaks to us directly through Psy Chic Anem One:

When we met by the river, the changing scenery did not make much difference to me. I continued travelling west towards the golden promise, untethered. I felt emancipated and feverish. I had not been caught, and it felt good to be alone. Committing such atrocious acts made me throw up several times; during them, but also later, when recalling them and replaying fragments.

I had known such loneliness. It became blue boredom, the kind of boredom that enables you to play mindlessly with a piece of stick for hours. To play with it till you end up perforating the palpitating flank of a grey jackrabbit, repeatedly hacking at its soft belly with the blunt end. The fur wet with blood.

In that boredom, you change your mind abruptly. You feel ashamed of yourself, repelled, and afraid of how that reflects on your relationship to the world. It makes you feel maternal and protective over this dying animal slumped in your once torturous, now benevolent hand. It is bleeding heavily, but you suddenly lack the compassion and courage necessary to kill it, to end the suffering and pain that you caused.

You try and resuscitate it, gently nursing the wound that you inflicted. You weep with remorse, holding it against your face in a moment of wild delusion, thinking that you could bring some kind of comfort to this helpless animal. It is terrified of you. It knows and has known what you are capable of. It cannot physically escape you, your yawning cruelty, your unflinching capacity to refuse mercy, your resolve. It will die terrified of you and your desire to destroy it and then save it. It will die slowly because of your gutlessness, it will bleed to death, terrified in your idle hands, pressed against your body.

I suffered more, but also did worse.

Phenotypic plasticity.

You were a beautiful and precocious child. You came to me by the water. I was caked in dirt.

Later, you sobbed till your nose bled and begged me to kidnap you.

Yes, just like you, I once was epic.

ACKNOWLEDGEMENTS

For Yael, Ariela, Rod, Oedipuss; my family. And the ghosts.

Thank you Rebecca Jagoe, and Flo Ray for taking these ectoplasmic expressions and making them communicative.

Strange Attractor Press 2019